MW01195032

Cover Photography by Wander Aguiar Photography

Cover Design and Interior Format
© The Killion Group Inc.

To Kim—

ON HIS
Knees

Find your forever!

XO, Laura Kaye

NEW YORK TIMES BESTSELLING AUTHOR

LAURA KAYE

Praise for the Blasphemy Series

"Laura Kaye shows her mastery of the BDSM world. I'm eagerly anticipating more in this bold new series!"

~ Cherise Sinclair, *NYT* Bestselling Author of the MASTERS OF THE SHADOWLANDS SERIES

"Smoldering and sexy, Laura Kaye's Blasphemy series is everything I look for in a romance. Haunted heroes and strong heroines populate this one of a kind club and I can't wait to see the big bad Doms fall one by one."

~ Lexi Blake, *NYT* Bestselling Author of the MASTERS AND MERCENARIES SERIES

Hot Contemporary Romance by Laura Kaye

Warrior Fight Club Series
FIGHTING FOR EVERYTHING - May 22, 2018
FIGHTING FOR WHAT'S HIS - August 2018
FIGHTING THE FIRE - October 2018

Blasphemy Series
HARD TO SERVE
BOUND TO SUBMIT
MASTERING HER SENSES
EYES ON YOU
THEIRS TO TAKE
ON HIS KNEES

Raven Riders Series
HARD AS STEEL
RIDE HARD
RIDE ROUGH
RIDE WILD
RIDE DIRTY – March 13, 2018

Hard Ink Series
HARD AS IT GETS
HARD AS YOU CAN
HARD TO HOLD ON TO
HARD TO COME BY
HARD TO BE GOOD
HARD TO LET GO
HARD AS STEEL
HARD EVER AFTER
HARD TO SERVE

Hearts in Darkness Duet
HEARTS IN DARKNESS
LOVE IN THE LIGHT

Heroes Series
HER FORBIDDEN HERO
ONE NIGHT WITH A HERO

Dedication

To finding where you belong.

Chapter 1

IT WAS ENTIRELY POSSIBLE THAT Alex McGarry was too damn old for this shit.

That was his thought just before he stepped under the scalding hot spray of the shower. Bracing a hand against the marble tile, he bowed his head and let the water rain down on the back of his neck. He held the position for a long while, hoping the heat would ease the knot of muscle there, the knot borne from the exertion of whipping a submissive—and from learning the hard way that the woman hadn't been entirely honest about her limits.

Something made clear when the submissive had safeworded out of the scene, tears and a half-horrified accusation in her eyes.

Sonofabitch.

Alex had been fucking up too much lately. A few months back, with Master Wolf's submissive, Olivia, when Alex had invited her ex-fiancé to Blasphemy at an open house at the club. He hadn't realized they had a history, but that didn't absolve him from the guilt he felt about the horrible confrontation that'd gone down when the guy made a move on Liv. And now, tonight, with this submissive.

He should've been able to read her. How had he missed it?

Having been a part of Blasphemy since its beginning, Alex had seen it grow from a mere idea trying to take root in the ruins of an abandoned church, to it becoming the hottest club in Baltimore, one that drew players from as far away as New York and Richmond—and beyond. After all these years, things should be easier.

But here he was, a few weeks shy of his fortieth birthday. Still trying to figure shit out. Still able to feel shamed about being a sadist. Still alone.

That last one was getting to him more and more every damn day.

Enough with the pity party.

Tilting his head back, he closed his eyes and scrubbed the spray of water over his face.

Yeah. Enough.

Alex wrapped a towel around his waist and made his way into the locker room. The area wasn't huge—for there were only twelve Master Dominants who co-owned Blasphemy and shared this private lounge that overlooked the club's main space—but it was well appointed, with mahogany paneling, soft leather sofas and chairs, and a few private spaces in case one of the Masters wished to spend the night.

It was so late that Alex was surprised to find someone else there, sitting on the long bench in between the two walls of lockers—and he was even more surprised by who it was.

"Hale?" Alex said, able to identify the man from the multitude of tattoos that covered his skin even though he sat with his head in his hands. "I didn't realize you were here tonight." In fact, he wasn't sure when he'd last seen Hale O'Keeffe at the club. Maybe at the masquerade ball back in October? Hale owned the largest share in Blasphemy, and once upon a time had nearly lived at the club. That was back at the beginning, when they'd all had to pitch in more to get the business up and running. But it made Hale's more recent absences stand out to Alex and the other Masters—absences they'd all privately wondered about.

Almost like he was moving in slow motion, Hale peered over his shoulder and gave a small smile. "Got here late," he said, his voice nearly a raw scrape, as if he were exhausted.

Standing at his locker, Alex traded his towel for a pair of boxers. "You doing okay?" he asked, even though the answer seemed pretty damn obvious.

Hale tugged on a long-sleeved black T-shirt and rose as he answered. "You know, I don't even know. I've just been…off. It's nothing."

Eyeballing the guy, Alex debated whether to push. He was a psychiatrist, but that didn't mean people wanted to be analyzed every time they talked to him. Sometimes people just needed to vent or commiserate, no probing questions asked. But there was something about the set of Hale's shoulders that made it seem like he carried the weight of the world there. And his once jet-black hair was now shot through with some gray. So, Alex came down on the side of pushing. "You sure? Anything you want to talk about?"

"Nah. Nothing a good night of sleep won't cure, you know? But thanks," he said, giving a more genuine smile.

Alex nodded. "I know how that is," he said. "So get the hell out of here then."

Hale chuffed out a laugh. "Yeah, yeah. You come by your hard-ass reputation honestly, you know that?" He winked and threw a wave. "Good night."

"Night," Alex called, stepping into his pants, then his shirt, then his shoes. In Hale's absence, the locker room felt even more quiet. And in all that silence, Alex's thoughts sounded that much louder. Thoughts that the somewhat strange encounter with the other Dom stirred up even more. Because if he wanted to admit it, Alex saw something of himself in the haggard demeanor Hale had briefly let show.

Damnit, he was all up in his head tonight, wasn't he?

Once, all this gave Alex such a pure, visceral contentment. The club, the BDSM lifestyle, finding partners who craved his brand of sexual sadism—*once*, it'd left him energized on a fundamental level, even when the physicality of it had exhausted his body. It was always a *good* kind of tired.

Now?

Now part of him felt like Hale had looked, sitting there with his shoulders rounded, his head in his hand. And on that note, Alex slammed his locker door and made his way out.

Downstairs, he found the main floor of the club empty. Or mostly empty, anyway. Because Masters Quinton Ross, Wolf Henrikson, and Kyler Vance were still there, sitting around the circular iron-and marble bar that dominated the center of the old church's nave with a bottle and three glasses between them.

"Oh, hell yeah. Pour me one," Alex said as the others called out a greeting. Maybe it made him an asshole, but he was relieved that none of the other Dom's submissives were there. All three men were in committed relationships, and Alex was happy for them. Any other night he wouldn't have minded the ladies' company. But the fact that quite a few of the other Blasphemy Masters had paired off over the course of the last year highlighted

Alex's inability to find someone of his own. Tonight, he didn't need the reminder.

"Rough night, man?" Quinton asked, pushing a tumbler of amber liquor his way.

Alex gave a humorless laugh as he swirled the liquid in his glass. "Had a submissive bite off more than she could swallow and safeword out of a scene."

"Shit," Kyler said, brows cranking down over bright blue eyes.

Among these three Doms, Kyler's kinks aligned most closely with his own, with both of them having interests that extended down the edgier end of the spectrum. And he and Kyler also worked in fields that made their edge play even riskier—Kyler as a detective on the Baltimore City police force and Alex in the mental health field. If word got out that either of them were into the shit they were into, it could have repercussions much bigger than a scene gone bad. It was part of the reason all players at the club had to sign non-disclosure agreements.

"Sorry to hear that," Kyler said. "But what the hell was she thinking? It's not like your interests aren't perfectly well known around here."

True enough. Alex occasionally did public demonstrations with one of a handful of regular submissives, men and women, who came to him to sate their masochism. He had an intimidating reputation around the club—intimidating as much because of his standoffish demeanor as because of the pain he could inflict, for those who were into that sort of thing.

"Don't beat yourself up, man. It happens," Wolf said, throwing him a sympathetic look. "Hopefully she learned something important about understanding her own limits."

"I'll drink to that," Alex said, raising his glass. They

clinked, and then he was throwing back the whiskey and relishing the bite as he swallowed it down. "So, I saw Hale was here."

"Yeah, he passed through a few minutes ago," Quinton said, leaning against the counter from inside the circular bar. The club's food and beverage manager, the guy was also their most popular bartender. "We invited him to stay but he waved us off."

The four of them traded quiet looks for a moment. Kyler was the first to break the tension. "Something's off with him."

Nodding, Alex said, "I asked. He downplayed it."

Wolf shrugged. "Before I met Liv, I'll be honest, I'd been questioning things. Whether I still belonged here. Whether the fact that I'd even ask such a question meant I might not be doing right by the submissives I played with. I think we all go through ups and downs with the lifestyle."

"Damn, man," Quinton said. "You never said anything."

"Honestly, I wasn't sure what to say. Or whether saying it would make you all question my commitment to what we've built here. But Liv helped me work that shit out." Wolf winked, his green eyes flashing.

Alex was as surprised as he was relieved to hear Wolf's admission. And as Kyler and Quinton joined in with the man in singing the praises of their submissives, Alex's thoughts spun on what Wolf had said.

On the one hand, maybe it wasn't so unusual to be questioning things. Among the twelve Blasphemy Masters, only Hale was older than Alex or been in the community longer. But on the other, Wolf's cure for that questioning led Alex right back to the desire to find some kind of commitment amidst the kink. He didn't need every sexual encounter to be defined by his sadism, but he also couldn't live without it. That made it challenging to find play partners—let alone a potential long-term relationship—outside the lifestyle, or even outside Blasphemy.

Just so you know, I would seriously get off on your pain.

Yeah, that wasn't first-date material. Or even fifth date material.

For fuck's sake.

Alex threw back a gulp of the whiskey, then returned the glass to the bar top with more force than he'd intended. Three pairs of eyes cut his way.

"Sorry," he said. "I'm obviously shit for company." Kyler eyeballed him a little too closely, making him feel exposed. Exactly what he didn't need. Alex tugged on his coat. "I'm gonna head out, but thanks for the drink and the commiseration."

"Any time, man," Quinton said. "See you soon. And, oh, don't forget—"

Turning back, Alex halted. "About?"

"We need to know what you want to do for the New Year's Eve Party."

Damn. That was the second time Quinton had reminded him. The party was in less than two weeks. It wasn't at all normal for Alex to drag his feet on figuring out what he wanted to do for a demonstration, and it bothered him that he'd been so indecisive this time. Just one more brick in the wall of what'd been unsettling him lately. "I'll get on this tomorrow, Q. Sorry to make you ask twice."

"Not a problem, Alex. You know that. Have a good night."

With a single nod, Alex retreated across the long expanse of the club. In the quiet, his footsteps echoed up to the soaring ceiling of the old church with its stained-glass windows and stone pillars. Something about that reverberating sound made him feel so fucking alone despite the men he'd just left behind. The ride home, past festive store displays and light-bedecked houses, only added to that feeling of solitude, as did stepping into the quiet dark of his empty house.

Without turning on a light, he shrugged out of his coat, let it drop to the floor, and sank into the sofa. Kicked off his shoes and propped his feet up on the big coffee table. Closed his eyes.

He'd sleep right there tonight. So he didn't have to face being alone in his bed.

Chapter 2

"THIS ISN'T WORKING."

The sweat hadn't even dried on Jamie Fielding's skin when Liz's resigned pronouncement rang out from the other side of the mattress. His head swiveled against the pillow, and his gaze collided with that of the woman he'd been inside of three minutes before and dating for the past two months. There was a matter-of-factness in the cast of her brown eyes that cut through all the bullshit. He couldn't challenge what she'd said, because he felt it, too. So instead, he agreed. "I wanted it to work."

Her smile was a little sad as she pulled the sheet up over her nakedness. "I know."

Jamie hated himself just a little for failing at another relationship. Liz was smart and beautiful, successful and well-regarded in the advertising field. What more could a man want?

Yeah, what more, Jamie?

The gut check told him there was an answer to his question. He just hadn't found it. And he had no idea how to figure it out, either.

"I'm going to grab my stuff," she said, shifting to the

bed's edge.

He lowered his gaze, giving her a little privacy to make her way to the bathroom. Jamie pulled on a pair of jeans and a shirt, scrubbed his hands over his close-cropped beard, and rolled his neck. What the hell was so screwed up inside him that he couldn't connect with people the way he wanted?

Once sex got involved, it was like his body turned off... or wouldn't turn all the way on. Sometimes he could only keep an erection or achieve orgasm by imagining... other scenarios. Darker scenarios. His mind wanted the sex to be good, and he wanted to stay in the moment, but there was always something missing. And it left him feeling like there was a wall between him and his partners even when he was as physically close as two people could get.

So this failed relationship—and all the ones that'd come before—he *knew* they were his fault. Which was a sonofabitch because he had no idea what the fuck was wrong with him. And at twenty-nine, you'd think he'd have a goddamn clue.

From the adjoining room, little noises sounded out as Liz collected the few things she'd begun leaving at his place weeks before. A razor. Her toothbrush and toothpaste. A small bag with a brush and some makeup in it. She returned dressed, her arms full.

Awkwardness bloomed between them for a long minute until Jamie finally broke it with his words. "I'm sorry, Liz."

"Me, too," she said.

He gestured for her to go first out of the room, and he followed her downstairs. "Let me get you something to carry everything." He fished a handled shopping bag from the utility closet off the kitchen while she gathered more belongings that had migrated to his house. Canisters of her favorite tea and hot chocolate. A sweatshirt.

When she'd stowed everything in the bag, she stepped into her boots and tugged on her coat. An empty regret parked itself in Jamie's gut, but what was truly sad about the sensation was that he wasn't going to miss Liz so much as he was going to miss the potential feeling of belonging that Jamie couldn't seem to find. With anyone. Which meant that Liz deserved so much more than him.

Standing at his back door, she gave him a last lingering look. "Well, take care of yourself."

"You, too," he said, opening the door for her. Cutting December air blasted in around the storm door.

Just when he thought she'd take flight, she leaned back in. "I hope you find whatever it is you're looking for. Merry Christmas, Jamie."

For a moment, the sentiment hit him like a punch to the gut. What *was* he looking for? "Merry Christmas, Liz," he managed. But she was gone before he even finished the sentence.

Then Jamie was all alone with her parting words ringing in his ears. He blew out a long breath and secured the door. Braced his hands against the kitchen counter and stared at the multi-colored speckles in the granite surface. Paced to the fridge and stared blankly inside.

Restlessness flashed through him. No way did he want to sit around here thinking about Liz's question while staring at the little artificial Christmas tree they'd put up in his front window. Thank fuck he was flying out to his parents' place in California in one week's time—the change of scenery would do him good. Except for the part where he had to answer his mother's questions about how his relationship was going.

Shit.

He needed to get out of here—to do *something*. A quick glance at the clock on the microwave revealed it was still early enough on a Saturday evening to hope—so he picked up the phone and made a call.

A man's voice answered. "Hard Ink Tattoo. Can I help you?"

"Hey Jeremy, it's Jamie Fielding."

"Yo, Jamie. What's up, man?" Jeremy Rixey asked, his tone full of his characteristic good humor. Jamie had gone to the guy for all of his ink for the past five years, and they'd long since moved from a business relationship to friendship. "Tell me I get to work on you again soon."

Grinning, Jamie nodded. "That's why I'm calling. I know it's a long shot but any chance you have an opening tonight?"

"Someone's missed me, I see."

Jamie rolled his eyes and smirked. Jeremy was one of the most flirtatious people he'd ever met, and the guy flirted equally with women and men alike—and everyone seemed drawn to him in return. Jamie sure always had been, but Jeremy was one of those people that made you feel good to be around. "Well, I've missed your tattoo gun, at least."

A dark chuckle rolled down the line. "Aw, dude, now I'm even more flattered. My gun missed you, too."

Jamie guffawed, and heat crawled into his cheeks. Jeremy always managed to get to him this way. Maybe that was odd given that he was straight, but Jamie couldn't deny Jer's ability to push his buttons. "That's not— I mean, damnit."

"Walked right into that one, Fielding. Admit it."

"Yeah, yeah. Can you fit me in?" he asked, more than a flustered and exasperated. The whole thing with Liz had him on edge.

In the background, Jamie could just make out the sound of Jeremy's fingers moving against a keyboard. "Hmm, for you I can be open around eight, if that's not too late. But I promised Charlie that I'd be free by nine thirty tonight. How big of a piece are you thinking?"

"I want to expand the shoulder tattoo onto my back, so I'm flexible about how much we do." Because as much as Jamie genuinely did want more of the cool blue-and-black tribal that formed a sleeve covering the entirety of his left arm, he wanted the bite of the tattoo gun even more. Tonight, that biting pain mattered more than the design that gave it to him.

"Okay, then you got it. See you at eight?"

Satisfaction flooded through Jamie's gut. "Yeah, man. Thanks."

Restless as Jamie was, it took forfuckingever for eight o'clock to roll around, and then he was parking his Range Rover at the curb in front of the big warehouse building that Hard Ink Tattoo called home. You'd never know from the neighborhood, filled as it was with abandoned buildings, that the city's preeminent tattoo shop was located here.

A buzzer screeched above his head as Jamie stepped into the shop. His gaze scanned over the colorful images that covered every inch of wall space, a mix of tattoo design templates and finished pieces that Jeremy and his other artists had completed. It only took Jamie a minute to find the photo of one of his own tattoos, one he wore on the outside of his right calf that made it look like he had a mechanical skeleton beneath his skin.

Footsteps sounded out from the hallway that extended from behind the reception desk, and Jamie turned to see Jeremy, a big grin on his face, his brown hair a wavy, finger-raked mess, his pale green eyes full of humor. In full

Jeremy Rixey style, he wore a T-shirt with a goofy-looking orange squirrel that read, *Come Play With My Nuts.*

Jamie chuffed out a laugh. "Jeremy, how the hell are you?"

Jer flicked his tongue over the twin piercings on his bottom lip. "Never better," he said, extending his hand. They shook.

"First time I've seen you since your big news," Jamie said, referring to his engagement to a man he'd been dating for the past year or so. "Congratulations."

A grin nearly split the guy's face. "Thank you."

"When's the big day?" Jamie asked, happy for his friend even as a part of him wondered what it would feel like to find the kind of connection with another person that would make someone look that joyful and content.

"May. And then we're going to go somewhere warm where pants are optional."

Jamie chuckled. "That's life goals right there."

Waggling his eyebrows, Jeremy nodded. "Tell me about it. But enough about me. It's been too long since I've seen you. What? Two, three months?"

Yup. And that time frame was…not a coincidence, was it? He'd last been here just before he met Liz… "Yeah, sounds about right."

"Well, it's good to see you again. Come on back. You know the drill."

"Quiet in here tonight," Jamie said. He was used to music playing. Or to Jer's soon-to-be-married employees, Ike and Jess, bantering with each other. Sometimes, there was even a three-legged German shepherd who hung out in the shop, wreaking havoc with a squeaky tennis ball or by stealing things from Jess, whom the dog seemed to love to goad into playing chase.

"Ike and Jess had a thing tonight, and I'd blocked out

my schedule with drawing time for a big back piece I'm starting tomorrow." Jer led them into his tattoo room and gestured to the chair sitting in the middle of the room.

"Aw, hell. You shoulda pushed me off, man," Jamie said, shrugging out of his coat.

"Nope, no need. I got it done. Wanna see?"

"Hell, yeah." Jamie followed Jer out into the big square lounge at the back of the shop. An abstract spray-painted mural dominated the rear wall, reading, *Bleed with me and you will forever be my brother.* Something about the sentiment appealed to Jamie on a visceral level and had for as long as he'd been coming here.

Several round tables filled the center of the floor, and on one sat a stack of books, a sprawl of art supplies, and several versions of a huge design. One was clearly Jeremy's original full-color hand drawing, and the second was a black-and-white image that would become the stencil from which Jeremy would outline the actual tattoo. It was a dozen-panel superheroes-against-villains comic strip, without words. And though it wasn't to Jamie's taste, the artistry and boldness of it were freaking awesome. "This is incredible, Jeremy."

"Yeah?" Arms crossed, he stood studying it. "I keep making little adjustments."

Jamie leaned closer. "How long will this take you? It looks damn intricate."

Jeremy braced his hands on the back of a chair, bringing them shoulder to shoulder as they studied the piece. "Probably three or four sittings depending on the guy's tolerance for pain."

A jolt of heat flashed through Jamie's body, and he found himself slanting a gaze at the other man.

Jer grinned and winked. "Not everyone can handle the burn the way you can."

Out of nowhere, arousal slinked through Jamie's body. Flushing, he forced his gaze back to the drawing. But he could barely see it for the riot currently erupting inside his brain. Where the hell had this reaction come from? And what exactly was he reacting *to*? Jeremy's words? Jeremy himself? The idea of how much a big full-color tattoo could hurt?

Or D) All of the above, a little voice in his brain whispered. Because he had occasionally gotten aroused from getting inked before, though he'd always chalked it up to the adrenaline rush.

What the hell?

A hand slapped him on the shoulder. "Well, come on in and get naked for me. Time for me to get my hands on your back."

"Uh, yeah. Right," he murmured. But he lingered with the drawing for just another minute, because his body was so not under control, and he was kinda struck stupid trying to understand it. Maybe he was just on edge because of the break-up?

He approached the tattoo room like a snake might jump out at him, but only found Jeremy preparing his work station. Acting totally normal. Seemingly unaware that he'd just inspired arousal in a man who two hours ago had been inside a woman. A *straight* man. A straight man whose gut clenched with a foreign, anxious heat as he removed his shirt and straddled the chair.

What. The. Hell.

Jamie had never been the kind of man who couldn't acknowledge that another man was good-looking, but he'd never had this kind of physical reaction to another man before, had he? A memory came out of nowhere, of getting hard listening to his college roommate masturbate in the darkness of their shared space, when Ryan had thought Jamie was asleep. But he'd never thought that was so much about Ryan as about being a secret voyeur to someone else's pleasure.

Which all led Jamie back to *what the hell…*

Fortunately, the first sharp vibration of the tattoo gun against his shoulder chased a lot of the angsty overthinking away, and then a little bit more, until Jamie relaxed into the burn of the needles against his skin. The outlining wasn't too painful, though his tribal had nice, thick outlines that meant Jer had to go over the same stretch of skin again and again until his nerve endings fucking sang. But the filling in with color, *that* was where things got really good. Where the concentrated focus of the gun made him feel nearly high with an explosion of endorphins.

Part of Jamie wished it hurt even more, because maybe then he'd fly even higher.

This was why he loved getting a tattoo. This was why he had a full sleeve on one arm, a biceps piece on his other arm, a rib tatt that'd hurt like hell, the mechanical leg on his calf, and another tribal on the back of his leg. Together, they represented about twenty-two hours' worth of work.

Twenty-two hours' worth of pain.

Thinking about it that way, something inside him stirred with an odd sort of satisfaction.

Jeremy made small talk as he worked, and while Jamie responded, the bigger part of his brain was offline riding the high. His thoughts were scattered and indistinct, a stream of consciousness inspired by the sensations flooding through him. Which was probably why his mind meandered back to his bedroom earlier, to being with Liz. *Why couldn't it have felt like this?*

The errant thought sent blood rushing to his dick.

"What's that?" Jeremy asked, wiping away excess ink as he expanded the big tribal onto Jamie's upper back.

"What?" Jamie asked. Heat bloomed over his cheeks, slow but steady.

"Dude, you just asked why something didn't feel like this." The tattoo gun worked over the same area of skin, the concentration evidence that Jer was filling in with color. And between the pain and the feeling of the man's big hands on his skin and the realization that Jer might catch him getting off on getting inked, Jamie's body couldn't decide whether to be aroused or embarrassed. Oddly, the combination of the two seemed to be doing… confusing things to him.

Jamie released a breath. "Oh, uh…" He shook his head and forced some of the haze away. "I dunno, man."

"You okay tonight?" Jer asked, a seriousness slipping into his tone.

He swallowed hard, his body pulled between competing emotions and reaction. So he gave voice to the only explanation he had for any of it. "Eh, yeah. Liz and I broke up."

"Aw, hell. I'm sorry," Jeremy said.

"Thanks. We weren't that serious. Anyway, I was just zoning out."

"Mmhmm. Zone away, my friend."

Heaving a deep breath, Jamie nodded. "Getting ink chases all the bullshit away, you know?"

Jer chuckled. "Amen to that. The pain is half the fun for you, isn't it?"

Jamie froze, then slowly turned his head to look over his shoulder at his friend. "Uh, yeah, I guess it is." His response came out sounding casual, but that belied the earthquake happening inside Jamie's brain.

I hope you find whatever it is you're looking for.

Liz's parting words came roaring back, but to what end? Jamie wasn't looking for pain, for fuck's sake. He had enough of that every freaking time a relationship went down in flames.

Jeremy threw him a wink. "Masochists are always good repeat customers for a tattoo shop."

Masochists? Wait, what?

"Knock, knock," came a man's voice from behind them, cutting off Jamie's chance to ask why Jer had made the leap all the way to that. Lots of people liked the burn of getting a tattoo, didn't they?

"Hey, babe," Jeremy said, finishing out a section of fill. "I'll be done in a few."

The tall, dark-blond-haired man lingered at the doorway. Charlie Merritt, Jeremy's partner and fiancé. They lived in a loft apartment on one of the upper floors of the building, so Jamie had met the guy before.

"Hey, Charlie," Jamie said. "You're welcome to come in."

Charlie gave a small smile as he moved closer. The guy was quiet and reserved but apparently scary brilliant when it came to computers. "Hi, Jamie. I didn't know you were coming by tonight."

"Last minute thing," he said. "Jeremy did me a favor."

Jer winked as he finished and cleaned the new tattoo. "I'm cool like that." He handed Jamie a mirror that confirmed, as expected, that the tribal looked all kinds of bad ass crawling down his back. It now went as far as his left shoulder blade in a series of blue-and-black arcs and zigzags.

Around the new design, Jamie's skin was bright red, and the evidence of the pain he'd endured—and would still endure as it healed—gave him a feeling of satisfaction, too.

"Awesome as always, man." Jamie turned from the wall mirror in time to catch Jeremy giving Charlie a kiss. Just a quick press of his lips against the corner of Charlie's smiling mouth. More affectionate than anything, but it still unleashed something inside Jamie.

Something that wanted what they so clearly had. The obvious love and chemistry that simmered beneath the surface of that little show of affection. Maybe it was strange that he looked at two men and saw what he wanted, but Jamie had always been struck by the strength of the connection that Jeremy and Charlie shared. Envious, even. So it didn't feel that strange to him to see in them what he wanted for himself.

"Let me get you bandaged," Jer said.

Jamie straddled the seat again, and as Jer rubbed ointment onto the new tattoo, Charlie gave a wave. "I'll let you finish up. Good to see you, Jamie."

"You, too, Charlie. And congrats on your engagement."

"Thanks," Charlie said, blushing and throwing Jeremy a crooked smile.

Taping on a bandage, Jer chuckled and winked. "Bye, babe. Be up in a few."

Jer made quick work of cleaning up while Jamie donned his shirt and coat. And then he was paying his bill at the front reception desk and shaking Jer's hand. "Thanks for working me in tonight. I needed it."

"Anytime, man. You know where to find me."

Jamie turned to go, then faltered. Debated. Turned back. "Actually, can I ask why you called me a masochist?"

Jer blinked, and a series of emotions ran over his expressive face. "Oh, uh. It's just that...some people get off on pain. I thought...well, am I wrong in thinking you're one of them?"

Jamie frowned. He absolutely *had* gotten off on the

pain tonight. There was no denying that. But still... "No. I've just never associated myself with being a masochist."

Jer's eyebrows rose to his hairline. "For real?" When Jamie only shrugged, the guy continued. "Well, hell, dude. Maybe you should look into it. Could be fun." He made a face full of innuendo and waggled his brows.

Goosebumps raced down Jamie's back, and his heart kicked up in his chest. "Look into it how?" he asked, and then he shook his head. "Is it weird we're having this conversation?"

Jeremy laughed. "Dude, I have no self-consciousness, trust me. Baltimore has a pretty big kink and fetish community. There are discussion boards you could look into, and there's even a club..." His expression went thoughtful and distant.

"What?" Jamie asked, needing Jer to finish that thought. Because it felt like he was on the precipice of something important here.

"There's this club called Blasphemy. I have a friend who belongs. One of the co-owners, actually." Jer nailed him with a stare. "I could put you two in touch and you could see if it interests you."

Blasphemy. Exactly what kind of club was it? Jamie didn't know, but he was sure as hell curious to find out. "Uh, yeah. Yes. That sounds...good," he managed. Jer already had Jamie's cell number, of course, but he took down his email address, too.

And then all Jamie could do was wait. And wonder. And hope that Jeremy's mystery friend called and told him what this Blasphemy place was all about.

Chapter 3

JAMIE WALKED INTO HIS TOWNHOUSE, made directly for his office, and booted up his laptop. And then he typed exactly one word into the search bar.

Masochist

The search engine helpfully highlighted a definition right at the top.

A person who derives sexual gratification from their own pain or humiliation.

Jamie's pulse kicked up and heat roared over his body, making him realize he hadn't taken off his coat. He ripped it off and dropped it to the dark floor beside his chair.

His gaze scanned down.

Masochism: The condition in which sexual or other gratification depends on one's suffering physical pain or degradation that is self-imposed or imposed by others.

Jamie swallowed hard and sat back heavily in the big leather chair.

Which was when he realized his dick was rock hard.

Jesus Christ.

Was this…could this be…was this why he always felt so distant when he was having sex? Because he'd been needing something more without being aware of what it was?

And all this time...could it really have been *pain* he'd been missing?

Pain and degradation, a little voice in his brain whispered.

He stared at the laptop for a long moment, and then his own voice broke the silence. "This is fucking nuts."

Wasn't it? Except then he remembered the dark, twisted images he sometimes latched onto to get himself there during sex...

Jamie adjusted himself—because nuts or not, his erection wasn't going away—and then he typed the name of a porn site into the search bar. A dozen movie previews played showing people engaged in various explicit acts—just none doing quite what he wanted to see. So he searched for *masochist* again.

A new screen of thumbnails popped up, with preview after preview showing dominant men tormenting women with various kinds of rough sex. Spanking, flogging, electroshocking, orgasm denial, clothes pins and nipple clamps, and so much more...

He watched snippets of them all, definitely intrigued, clearly still aroused, but not yet *connecting.*

Because the recipients of the pain were all women. His fingers flew over the keyboard again.

Masochist men.

The new search term brought an entirely different array of movies—this time, all the men were on the receiving end and the more dominant partners were women. Some with a rough, aggressive touch, some with a more teasing approach, and yet others more motivated by dishing out humiliation than pain.

Jamie shifted in his seat, and finally gave in to unzipping his jeans. Because the more he looked, and the more he thought about this—*really* thought about it—the harder he got. And as he watched parts of one video, then another, he found himself thinking back over his relationships.

Unquestionably, he'd always dated strong women, most of whom he'd met either through his engineering program, law school, or his work as a patent lawyer. Like Liz, a copyright lawyer at another firm he'd met through mutual friends, the women he'd been with were smart, professional, and ambitious. And he'd liked that about them. In the bedroom, however, it was clear more often than not that they'd wanted him to take charge…and he hadn't questioned it.

He stared at the video playing before him, of a man tied down to a bench seat while a woman jerked him off—to just before the point of orgasm. And then she'd back off, leaving the man moaning and writhing in frustration and pain. A pain she ratcheted up by jerking him off again, focusing only on the tip. Or by squeezing him hard at the base of his erection while tapping with more than a little force against balls held tight within a cock ring. She brought him to the brink of orgasm again and again. Applying hard slaps against the insides of his thighs when the man seemed to need help holding back. And when he finally lost it, the orgasm was epic, wringing every one of the man's muscles, coating his chest with a massive come shot, and leaving him limp and panting—and then nearly crying when the woman took pleasure in stroking his now spent and painfully over-sensitive dick.

Jamie had watched the whole thing with bated breath, and finally had to take his own cock in hand. The guttural moan that ripped out of him as he stroked himself revealed the depth of his arousal. And his body lurched far too close to orgasm *way* too fast. So Jamie squeezed himself tight, cutting off the urge with a pinching pain that make him suck in a breath through his teeth.

And damn if that didn't provide its own kind of arousal.

"Fuck," he rasped. He didn't want to come yet. He wanted to see more. Explore more. Consider more. If this was really him. And, if so, what he intended to do about it.

Breathing harder, he navigated back out to the other movies, where a pattern quickly became obvious. The men in these videos weren't just masochists, they were also submissives. And the women weren't just aggressive or into rough sex, they were more often than not Mistresses within the context of BDSM.

Did masochists also have to be submissives? Watching a few more movies led Jamie to believe that, on some level, the answer was yes. Because they were submitting to the treatment that delivered the pain and humiliation.

Which of course made him wonder, *am I submissive?*

Shit, he really didn't know.

But what he did know was that, as aroused as he was, he'd lost some of the connection he'd felt during the handjob videos once the videos focused more on the women fucking the men. It almost felt like someone had turned down the heat. But as he watched one woman ride a man she'd tied down and gagged, and then another fuck a guy's ass with a strap-on dildo, Jamie's arousal definitely became less urgent.

What was working for him? And what wasn't?

God, he could barely believe he was thinking through this as methodically as he might one of his patent cases. Trying to understand the evolution of an idea into an invention. Analyzing how and why a machine worked. Considering what rules and laws applied—and which didn't.

Seeing men on the receiving end of the pain had been hotter for him than when it was women.

So...maybe seeing men on both sides of the equation would be hotter, too?

The question gave him pause, especially as he remembered his surprising reaction to Jeremy earlier. Could he really be pushing thirty and just learning that it was possible for him to be turned on by men, too? Although, if he was just figuring out the masochist part, how was that any different from realizing he might be...what? Bi? Bi-curious, at the very least? Granted, he'd spent most of his twenties buckled down pursuing multiple graduate degrees and clerkships, and, more recently, pulling sixty- and seventy-hour weeks as a new associate at his law firm. And amid the busy-ness of everyday life, he'd never before had any reason to question his heterosexuality. Although maybe he should've, given how often his relationships had gone down in flames.

Still, it all left him feeling like he was arriving late to the party of his own sexuality. For fuck's sake.

No more questioning it. It was about time to figure this shit out. So he ran the search for gay porn involving rough, painful sex, his heart beating hard against his breastbone as images populated the screen. He scrolled until he found one that looked promising.

"Oh, Jesus fuck..."

Jamie's jaw fell open and his pulse raced as the scene unfolded. One man unexpectedly overpowered another. Forcibly removed his clothes. Shoved him to his knees. Choked him with his cock, making him learn to take it all. The dubious-consent element lessened as the man on his knees began thanking the other man for the abuse he dished out, both verbal and physical—although, Jamie had to admit, he'd found the part that had pushed the boundary of consent hot as fuck. And wasn't *that* something to file away for further consideration?

But it was the dominant man's roughness, his strength, his size, his ability to manhandle that Jamie found so appealing. God, to experience that... Just imagining it shoved Jamie hard toward the need for release.

By the halfway point of the clip, the submissive man endured weights hanging from his balls, the soft flogging of his straining cock and the much-harder flogging of his ass and back, and hard smacks of black-gloved hands against his pecs.

And Jamie realized he was squeezing his own cock so tight that he was sweating.

This. This worked for him. This worked for him in fucking *spades.*

All it took was the top flipping the bottom onto his back and shoving his cock deep into the other man's ass before Jamie absolutely had to jack himself off. Before his need was beyond urgent. Hard pinches of the man's nipples rushed sensation into Jamie's balls. But the thing that shoved him over the edge was when the dominant man grabbed hold of the throat of the man beneath him and choked off his air.

"*Fuck!*" Jamie roared into the emptiness of his office as his body detonated. "Fuckfuckfuck."

He collapsed back into his chair, unable to care about the mess he'd made. Unable to move.

Unable to make any sense of the fact that a gay sadomasochism porn scene had just made him come harder than he'd ever come in his whole life.

Unable to do anything...except accept that what he'd just watched had turned him on in a way little else ever had.

And pray that Jeremy's friend might somehow help Jamie find an opportunity to experience something like this in real life.

"I had an interesting conversation yesterday," Master Kyler said as he came up to the desk in Blasphemy's member registration office on Monday evening.

Alex looked up from where he'd been logging into the computer system. "Is this where I'm supposed to ask you what it was?" So, obviously, he was still in a mood. It'd been a shitty weekend, and the misstep with the submissive on Friday night still hung over him like a cloud.

Kyler smirked, not at all put off. "Yeah, motherfucker."

Okay, that eked a chuckle out of Alex. He stopped what he was doing and asked, "Please tell me about your interesting conversation, Master Kyler."

Now the guy grinned. "You know, you can be quite accommodating when you put your mind to it."

"Jesus, Ky," Alex said, chuffing out a laugh. The one problem with being a hard ass? The people who knew you best and saw through your façade also knew how to push your buttons—and took great pleasure in doing so.

"Okay, okay," he said, holding up his hands. He swung a chair around and straddled it backwards. "A good friend of mine owns a tattoo shop across town. Has a regular client who's become a friend and who's interested in the lifestyle. I had coffee with the prospective this afternoon."

Alex blinked. "Did we get to the interesting part yet?"

"The guy comes with my friend's highest personal recommendation and I got a good read off of him. Works as an attorney. And he's a masochist. Completely untrained, of course, but eager as fuck." Kyler arched an excited brow over those bright blue eyes.

Groaning, Alex shook his head. "I don't do newbies." It wasn't the ignorance of D/s protocol that Alex had a problem with, so much as it was how high the physical and psychological stakes were in a S&M scene, let alone a S&M relationship. Errors in protocol could offer some very useful grounds for creative correction. But Alex had had one too many conversations with self-styled masochists who really wanted the façade of sadism they saw Hollywood depict, which usually amounted to no more than garden-variety rough sex.

"I know, I know," Kyler said, holding up a hand. "And nobody says you have to scene with him. But maybe you could, I don't know, answer some questions? Show him around? Get him oriented to all this a little? As a favor to me."

"Sonofabitch. He's coming here tonight, isn't he?" Alex said.

Kyler's smile was one Alex had seen drive women to their knees. But it just made Alex want to punch something. "Told him to come around nine thirty."

Perfectly timed for Alex to be the one to in-process him before his shift at the registration desk ended. He gave Kyler a well-practiced stern stare, the kind that usually made a submissive drop his or her gaze to the floor.

"You want to beat the shit out of me right now, don't you?" The guy winked. Fucking *winked!*

"Desperately," Alex said.

Ky chuckled, rose, and swung the chair back into place. "Guy's name is Jamie Fielding. Thanks, man."

"I think you need a refresher course in consent, Vance," Alex said, his fingers taking out his frustration on the keyboard.

"You're a god among men, Master Alex," Kyler said,

walking backward toward the door to the club's main floor.

"I don't like you." Alex kept his gaze on the screen, but he could feel the humor radiating from the other man without looking. And then Kyler slipped into the club, leaving Alex alone to begin his shift at the membership registration desk, where the club processed the paperwork for all members, and issued color-coded and flagged cuffs to all submissives so that their availability and limits were knowable on sight. All of Blasphemy's Master Dominants took turns running various aspects of the club's operations, and without question their ownership of the club went way beyond the financial stake each of them had in it.

This place was a community for them. A lifestyle. A family, even.

So, fine, Alex would do Kyler this favor, not to mention his duty to the club, and give the guy a basic orientation. Besides, who better to make sure the man wasn't in over his head in billing himself as a masochist.

But, beyond that, he was *out.*

Chapter 4

AS JAMIE STEPPED FROM THE rear of the public Club Diablo and into the private courtyard that fronted a huge church, he felt like he'd walked through the back of a magical wardrobe and into a fantasy land that he'd never known existed. He never would've known this old church building was back here, located as it was behind a big renovated warehouse building, the quirk of some long-ago evolution in the city's development. Given the emphasis that Kyler—*Master* Kyler, he needed to get used to saying—had put on confidentiality, no doubt the hidden nature of the location was part of the point.

Jamie's breath frosted in puffs as it hit the cold December air, but underneath his coat, he was over-warm with anticipation and nervous excitement.

Forcing his feet to move again, he crossed the courtyard toward black double doors situated off to the side. A guard checked for his name on a list, then welcomed him inside.

Beyond the initial entry and waiting rooms, he was led into a registration room where he found a man sitting behind an ornate desk. A man who threw him a look that was momentarily so hard, so almost *mean*, that his pulse spiked and goosebumps rushed over his skin.

But Jamie must've imagined it, because then the man gave him a polite smile as he gestured to the chair opposite the desk. "You must be Jamie Fielding. Welcome to Blasphemy. Please have a seat."

"Thank you," Jamie said. He removed his charcoal wool pea coat and sat.

For a long moment, the other man studied him, and Jamie was too curious about everything not to study him right back. He was older than Jamie, had dark hair above even darker eyes, and possessed a face that appeared both distinguished and harsh. He wore a black button down with the sleeves rolled to mid-forearm, revealing a worn soft black leather cuff with an embroidered Gothic 'M' on his right wrist. And his gaze was so intense, so piercing, that it made Jamie's heart beat faster. He almost felt like they were locked in some sort of contest, one that Jamie was losing if the urge to look away—to look down—was any indication.

And then it occurred to Jamie, and he did look down. "Thank you, *Sir*." For as much reading as he'd spent the day doing—thanks to Master Kyler's recommendations after they'd had coffee—Jamie had forgotten the most basic aspect of the protocol here. "I'm sorry, Sir. I'm new. And nervous." And an idiot, apparently.

"You're fine, Jamie." But it did earn him a short, approving nod. "I'm Master Alex, and I'm going to get your provisional membership processed and give you an orientation to the club and its rules," the man said. "Did you bring the paperwork Master Kyler gave you?"

Nodding, Jamie pulled an envelope from the inside pocket of his coat and handed it over, once again chancing eye contact. "Yes, Sir. Everything's there." As a favor to

Jeremy, Master Kyler had arranged to sponsor Jamie for a provisional two-week membership. At the end of the provisional period, the head Masters would apparently vote on whether to extend him a regular membership. The only thing that sucked was that Jamie wasn't going to be able to make use of the whole two-week period given the week he was spending with his parents for Christmas. Still, it was an in that Jamie would've never gotten for himself, and he'd have to do something big to pay Jeremy back for having helped pull these strings.

Master Alex removed the paperwork from the envelope and unfolded it with an almost practiced precision. There was a rigidness about him that added to the veneer of his unapproachability. But at the same time, Jamie found the man utterly appealing precisely *because* of how damn intimidating he was.

Like he was a lion that might strike at any moment, beautiful but deadly.

Before this weekend, Jamie would've thought that was a strange reaction for him to have to another man, on so many levels. After a lifetime of considering himself straight, it was still a little confusing to realize he might've been wrong all this time. Or at least only half right? But thank God for the internet, because yesterday he'd spent time reading messages boards and learned that he wasn't alone in making it to his late twenties before realizing he might actually be bisexual. A few of the commenters talked about having a light-bulb moment when they first had the thought that they might not be straight, and Jamie identified with that a lot. Because his conversation with Jeremy had provided the first flash of insight that'd illuminated the possibility for him.

And now he wanted to explore these new sides of himself and see where they might lead.

Jamie relaxed as he answered a string of basic questions and absorbed the information Master Alex dispensed about protocol within the club. He explained that the cuff he wore marked him as one of Blasphemy's twelve Masters, who had final say about everything that happened at the club and who would serve as a resource for Jamie if he had questions or problems. He couldn't help but admire the way the soft black leather looked on the other man—not to mention being intrigued by what it represented.

Experience. Understanding. Mastery.

All qualities that'd turned Jamie on in those videos he'd watched. All things Jamie craved to have applied to himself.

Master Alex pulled a white cuff from a drawer. "Submissives wear their own cuffs. White for unattached, red for attached. No player should approach an attached submissive without his or her Dominant's permission. However, for unattached submissives, your cuff will allow Dominants to know your interests, and your limits." He pulled two sheets of paper from among those Jamie had given him.

Jamie swallowed hard. He knew what the sheets were. The first was a checklist of activities—sexual and otherwise—that he'd been asked to mark one of three ways: *willing to perform/experience*; *soft limit*, meaning open to experience but with reservations; and *hard limit*, meaning unwilling to perform/experience. The second was similar, but included a list of riskier activities defined as edge play that Master Kyler had given him to complete given his interest in masochism.

Having never done some of the acts, it hadn't been easy to determine how to mark some items, and Jamie had done more research—reading and porn—to judge what his reactions were.

Master Alex pulled a tray of colored ribbons from the drawer. "The different colors indicate your interests and limits." He held up two ribbons and arched a brow as he nailed him with a stare. "Light blue is for interest in moderate pain. Dark blue is for interest in intensive pain play."

Jamie's heart was suddenly a bass drum in his chest, especially with the way Master Alex studied him. The problem was, Jamie wasn't sure which to choose. His gut told him to go with the dark blue. Hell, his cock wanted the dark blue, too. But having never done this before, what if he was wrong? What if he couldn't take what he thought he wanted?

He swallowed hard. "Sir, may I ask your advice? Because I crave the dark blue, but being so new, I don't want to make a promise to a Dominant that I can't keep."

It took everything Jamie had to hold the other man's gaze, especially when a look of surprise flashed across his face.

Master Alex's gaze became more appraising, and he nodded. "Recognition of your limitations is always a strength, Jamie. In your case, your inexperience is a limitation. One you can overcome. Begin with the light blue."

"Yes, Sir," he said, glad he'd asked, even as a tendril of disappointment curled into his belly.

"This disappoints you," Master Alex said as he attached the light blue. It wasn't a question.

"A little, Sir."

He nailed him with a dark stare. "If this place, this lifestyle, is really for you, it's a marathon, not a sprint."

Jamie nodded, appreciating the reminder. And as other colored ribbons joined the first, excitement stirred anew in his gut. There was green for a willingness to engage in sex, orange for anal sex—even though Jamie'd never had it before, gold for group sex, and red for bondage.

Master Alex shifted to the list of edgier play, and knowing that the other man was reading about what kinds of things made up the gist of Jamie's darker, more deviant sexual fantasies had him suddenly rock hard in his jeans. As subtly as he could, Jamie adjusted himself. But he needn't have worried about being caught because Master's Alex's eyes remained on the page, allowing Jamie to look his fill at the other man.

Who was unquestionably attractive, not a little compelling, and seriously intimidating. Jamie had no idea what Master Alex was into, but after all Jamie's explorations of the past two days, it was like his brain—and his libido—were suddenly open to considering anything. Everything.

Knowing that Master Alex was learning Jamie's most secret inner desires had Jamie considering Master Alex's in return. Was this Dom interested in the humiliation, breath play, cock-and-ball torture, and consensual non-consent scenes that Jamie had indicated he was willing to do? Did he like electrical shock and medical play, which Jamie had indicated he might be willing to try? And how the heck did a submissive go about finding out what a Dom was interested in? Was it rude to ask?

Jamie didn't know. But apparently his body was unconcerned about the logistics, because having his deviancies laid out for another man to peruse rushed a wave of arousal through him and left him feeling like someone had taken a blowtorch to his blood.

That someone being the man with all the sharp edges sitting right in front of him. Master Alex. He didn't exactly know what to do with that fact, but that didn't make it any less true.

"This last ribbon will indicate an openness to edge play," Master Alex said, his voice tight, strained. "It will be up to you and any Dom you might play with to discuss the parameters of what you're willing to do. However, I caution you to really get to know a person before you consider pushing the boundaries of safe, sane, and consensual play." He worked a striped yellow and black ribbon onto his cuff.

"Yes, Sir," Jamie said, restlessness flooding through him and making it hard to sit still.

"That completes what we need to do here," Master Alex said. "There are lockers through the door behind you. Please stow your coat, wallet, keys, phone and the like and then I'll take you for a tour of the club."

Jamie rose. "Yes, Sir," he said, glad for the opportunity to move, to exorcise some of the energy making his nerves jangle and his heart beat fast. As he made for the door, he would've sworn he felt Master Alex's eyes on his back. And he found himself hoping that the man might give him more than just a tour…

Alone again, Master Alex blew out a long, hard breath. Because Jesus fucking Christ. Jamie Fielding had so strongly radiated a heady combination of urgent need and excited anticipation that it'd been nearly a physical presence in the room. If that hadn't been appealing enough, his asking for Alex's advice about the pain ribbon colors was evidence of a thoughtfulness, seriousness, and honesty that Alex couldn't help but appreciate.

And then there'd been Jamie's list of interests and limits, which closely matched most of Alex's own. Of course, the real proof of compatibility would be in learning the extent of the man's true tolerance for pain, but in his willingness and openness, Alex found someone with whom he seemed to be largely on the same page.

He wasn't sure whether to thank Kyler or throttle him for giving Jamie the edge play list to complete. Kyler was obviously trying his hand at a bit of matchmaking. And he didn't appreciate it at all. Not when the Dom knew that Alex preferred experienced players.

Frustration parked itself like a rock in his gut.

Which of course was the moment when Jamie returned to the registration area.

He made for the chair, but Alex shook his head, wanting to see just how submissive he was. Wanting to give the guy a little bit of a hard time. Wanting to toy with him…

"You will remain standing."

Jamie froze, his hands falling restlessly to his sides.

Taking his good old time, Alex rose, pushed in his chair, rounded the desk. And then he came to stand right in front of the other man.

The guy was hot as fuck. That couldn't be denied. He wore his brown hair short, both on his head and on his face, where he had a perfectly groomed beard and moustache. He'd gone basic with his clothing—just a pair of black jeans and a form-fitting black T-shirt. But all that black did was highlight the riot of color on his left arm, where he had a full sleeve of ink that began at his wrist and disappeared underneath the shirt. They were almost perfectly matched for height, which allowed Alex to hold his gray-eyed gaze and see just how eager he was. Christ, the guy was nearly vibrating with an excited energy that Alex had to admit was a little contagious.

He tried to remember when he'd last felt that kind

of overwhelming exhilaration and anticipation—about anything. And he honestly fucking couldn't pinpoint it.

"Feet shoulder-width apart," Alex said.

Jamie blinked, unprepared for the command and momentarily caught off guard. But he recovered fast and spread his stance.

Circling, Alex moved behind Jamie, enjoying the tension he saw fill the man's shoulder muscles. "Arms behind your back, right hand atop the left, fingers straight, thumbs interlocked." When he followed the instructions, Alex leaned in. "Good," he said just an inch from Jamie's ear. He'd meant to tease the man, but so close, Alex inhaled the cool, clean scent of Jamie's soap, and perhaps of whatever oil or conditioner he applied to his beard. The guy smelled mouthwateringly good, and Alex kinda wanted to beat his ass for it.

Swallowing hard, he returned so that they stood face to face. "This position, with your eyes held forward, is *at ease*. Unless a Dom gives you an alternate instruction, it is always a safe and respectful position to take if you are unsure what to do."

"Okay—"

"*Silence*," Alex said, stepping closer. "No speaking unless I ask you a direct question or give you permission to speak freely. Do you understand?"

Jamie's eyes went wide and he licked his lips. "Yes, Sir."

Alex nodded. "On your knees."

Responding faster this time, Jamie sank downward. And it was a heady fucking thing, watching a new submissive obey—and watching them find pleasure in the obedience. Alex didn't know if Jamie had read up on kneeling or if it was a coincidence, but he nearly nailed the position, settling with his knees spread, his feet tucked under his ass, and his hands palms down on his thighs.

Alex relished having the kid at his feet way more than he should. "Palms up, gaze down. This is the *waiting* position, which is also good when you've made a mistake and wish to display contrition. Now, look at me."

Jamie tilted his head back to reveal that those gray eyes were fucking blazing. Alex allowed his own gaze to travel downward, to where a bulge filled out the front of the man's black jeans. Jesus.

"Present me your right wrist," he said, hearing a rasp to his voice that Jamie would have no reason to notice. When he obeyed, Alex fastened the white cuff there.

"Thank you, Sir," Jamie said. He hadn't needed prompting, proving that the kid truly felt the gratitude rather than merely knowing that gratitude was to be expected.

Fucking Kyler and his goddamned favor. Because Alex was self-aware enough that he couldn't deny that Jamie Fielding pushed his buttons, just like the other Dom had probably suspected. "Rise. Inside the club, you will be respectful, but you may speak freely and ask questions as they occur to you."

Resuming the at ease position, Jamie nodded.

Alex arched a brow and gestured toward the door to the main floor of the club. "Welcome to Blasphemy."

Chapter 5

FEELING MORE THAN A LITTLE overwhelmed by having another man order him to his knees—and by having *liked* it, Jamie followed Master Alex into what had once been the interior of a church. The space was huge, with a soaring ceiling, tall stained-glass windows, and colorful frescoes on the walls. Marble columns and potted plants created semi-private seating areas, and a huge round bar dominated the center of the space. Driving music played against the din of conversation, laughter, and cries of ecstasy.

Which had Jamie noticing the people. Beautiful and ordinary, young and old, some wearing street clothes, some in fetish wear, some wearing little—or nothing—at all. From the corner of his eye, he spied a woman on her knees giving a man a blow job while he stroked her hair and engaged in a conversation with other people in nearby seats. Around an X-shaped piece of furniture, a crowd gathered to watch a woman flog a naked man from chest to thighs and back again.

And he thought he'd been overwhelmed before. Jamie swallowed hard, trying to take it all in, but his senses were on overload.

"That's a Saint Andrew's Cross," Master Alex said. "It restrains a person in a spread-eagle position, as you can see."

Jamie nodded, embarrassed that his attention was held so rapt but at the same time unable to look away. The heat of a blush filled his cheeks, something brought home all the more when Master Alex whispered in his ear.

"You're blushing. No need to feel embarrassment. Mistress Dyan's submissive is an exhibitionist. He gets off on you watching."

Jamie looked at the Dom beside him, wondering what *he* got off on. "It just takes a bit of adjustment to seeing people being so open."

Master Alex tilted his head. "Are you shy, boy?"

Boy. How was it possible for that word to both make him bristle and turn him on? Because the ache in his cock told him the latter was true. "Not normally, Sir." Wanting to prove it, he asked the question that had been on his mind. "May I ask how a submissive learns what a Dom's into?"

Master Alex arched a brow over narrowed eyes. The look was meant to be intimidating, and it was. But it was also sexy as fuck. Truth be told, Jamie wanted to see it while he was pinned beneath the man. "It's not a submissive's place to initiate play. Doms will come to you and discuss…scenarios. But since you're new and I understand that you're trying to get your bearings, I'll also offer this. Getting to know the other submissives will be useful to you. They have a lot to teach you, including helping you get to know the other players and their reputations."

Jamie nodded, appreciating the advice. The flogged man cried out, drawing his attention back to the scene unfolding at the cross. Mistress Dyan wore a black leather corset and skirt over thigh-high black boots, and she wielded the flogger like it was an extension of herself. Naturally. Confidently. Unrelentingly.

He'd been half-erect since he'd walked through Blasphemy's door, but imagining being on the receiving end of the Domme's flogging had his cock getting hard again. So...both Master Alex and Mistress Dyan aroused him? Was it their dominance? Their ability to inflict pain? It seemed so, and it made him increasingly certain—he was aroused by the idea of both a woman and a man dispensing the pain. He was aroused by both women and men.

"Come," Master Alex said, stepping away and expecting Jamie to follow.

He blinked out of his thoughts and did as he was told, his brain unhelpfully imagining the man giving that command under entirely different circumstances. Jesus.

They approached the big bar, and the crowd parted a little as Master Alex leaned in. It was interesting to watch how others reacted to the Dom. With respect, deference, even something that looked a little like trepidation in a few people's eyes. In other *submissives'* eyes.

Jamie could confirm that the two women standing behind the closest seat were submissives by the cuffs on their wrists. But what he most noticed about them was how quickly they dropped their gazes in response to Alex's appearance. From under her lashes, the closest woman peered at Jamie, a curious, appraising look in her eyes. Like maybe she was wondering what kind of person would be with *this* Dominant.

Master Alex waved down the bartender, a brown-haired man with a quick smile, a booming laugh, and an easy-going demeanor that was exactly Alex's opposite. "Master Quinton, I'd like to introduce you to Jamie, a new prospective member."

The new Dom braced his hands on the counter, revealing the same black leather wrist cuff that marked him as one of the Masters of Blasphemy. "Jamie, welcome. I hope Master Alex is treating you well." Master Quinton winked, like he'd just included Jamie on an inside joke.

"Yes, Sir," he said, unable to hold back a smile around the man. There was something about him that was welcoming and relatable, like he was just a regular guy with whom you might hang out.

"Well, you need anything, you just let me know." Master Quinton grinned as he got called to the other side of the bar.

"I'll do that. Thank you, Sir."

"This way," Master Alex said, leading them around the bar. On the far side was a large dance floor and beyond it, a stage where the church's altar used to be. Instead of dancing, a crowd was assembled watching what appeared to be a show.

"Is this a bondage demonstration, Sir?" he asked, mesmerized by the fluid way the big Dom worked bright blue rope around the lithe body of a suspended blond woman.

Master Alex nodded. "Shibari rope bondage. Master Griffin is an expert at it."

Jamie watched as the new Dom created intricate knots and beautiful webs with the rope, as if the way it looked was as important as the way it restrained. "It's striking." He did a double take upon realizing that Master Alex was watching him watch the demonstration, his gaze narrowed and intense. Jamie dropped his own gaze. "I'm sorry, Sir. Did I say something wrong?"

Stepping closer, Master Alex nudged Jamie's chin, forcing him to look up. "Let me assure you that you'd have no question about that if it were the case. It is a Dom's prerogative to look at you. And I was enjoying looking."

A blast of heat rolled over Jamie, and he swallowed hard. What was it about this man that affected him so? Objectively, Masters Kyler and Quinton were attractive men, as was the big Dom on the stage, but Jamie hadn't lusted over any of them. Meanwhile, a single cutting look, or a sternly quiet sentence, when issued by Master Alex, nearly had the power to drive Jamie to his knees.

A thought that reminded him how hot it'd been to kneel at this Dom's feet. Why it was so sexy, Jamie wasn't sure, but he'd loved something about the way Master Alex had loomed over him, commanded him, made him feel safe and vulnerable at the same exact time.

"Yes, Sir," Jamie managed, not sure what else to say in response. And more than a little intrigued that Alex apparently enjoyed what he saw when he looked at him. He lifted his gaze to the stage again, and curiosity unleashed a question that Jamie hadn't intended to ask. "Do you ever do demonstrations, Master Alex?"

The Dom slanted him a glance. "I do."

A smile tugged at the corner of Jamie's mouth, because everything seemed to be a competition of wills with Alex, and somehow that managed to be funny and frustrating and infuriating and sexy all at the same time. "On anything in particular?"

Master Alex leaned in again and put his mouth to Jamie's ear. "Oh, my tastes are quite particular, boy."

There was that *boy* again. The warmth of the man's breath ghosted over Jamie's skin, unleashing a shiver in its wake. Licking his lips, Jamie peered at the other man, wondering just how hard he could push before he crossed a line. "Are they, Sir?"

One eyebrow arched in a tiny gesture that communicated so much. Caution. Challenge. Maybe even a little agitation. It *should've* made Jamie back off, but instead it kinda made Jamie want to know what would happen if he crossed one of Master Alex's lines.

Actually, Jamie wanted to know that *bad*.

But Master Alex withdrew, just a little, not taking the bait. And leaving Jamie feeling more than a little bereft. "Let's move on," he said, gesturing for Jamie to join him as they moved behind the crowd of onlookers toward a hallway that extended off the side of the space. The Dom stopped just short of entering it. "Typically, you wouldn't venture down here without invitation or chaperone, but for your information, this is where most of the private and themed play rooms are located."

Jamie peered down the wide stone hallway, and could only make out dark, heavy-looking doors spaced at regular intervals. He couldn't help but wonder what lay behind them. And whether he'd ever find out. More than that, whether he was *ready* to find out.

Master Alex made quick work of the remainder of the tour, pointing out bathrooms and seating areas, and introducing him to a few submissives, namely two ladies named Mia and Cass, who apparently belonged to Master Kyler and Master Quinton.

But Jamie got the distinct impression that Master Alex was suddenly rushing to finish the tour. Gone was the lingering and teasing and feeling that they were locked in some sort of battle of wills, and in its place was a purely professional Alex who seemed eager to finish his task and move on.

It was an impression that was confirmed when Master Alex led them back to the circular bar and asked, "Any last questions, Jamie?"

Jamie frowned, feeling something slipping away. Something maybe he never really had at all. But at the very least, there'd been some possibility. Some possibility of learning even *more* from Master Alex. He blinked and finally asked, "I don't think so. But what now, Sir?"

"Now, you decide if you want to play," Master Alex said. "And wait for a Dom to invite you to do so."

Alex stood at the one-way windows that comprised a whole wall of the Masters' lounge and looked out at the activity of the club below. He'd left Jamie at the bar fifteen minutes before and was glad to be free of the task of introducing him to Blasphemy.

Glad to be free of the fucking *temptation.*

Because Alex *had* been tempted. By the sub's curiosity, by his arousal, by his eager interest in everything. By the way Jamie seemed to flirt with pushing Alex—he would've sworn that was true. Either way, excitement had radiated off of the younger man, and Alex had to admit it was a heady, seductive thing to be reminded of the way all of this had once felt. Back at the beginning, when it was fresh and new and set his mind and his body on fire.

But at the same time, it was Jamie's newness that gave Alex pause. Because Jamie's ignorance and naiveté, not to mention the journey of sexual self-discovery the guy was clearly taking, all meant that not even Jamie was yet sure who or what he was, what he wanted, what he *needed.*

Which threw up red flags for Alex. Who wanted someone who'd accepted his own masochism and Alex's sadism. Who wanted the chance at a long-term relationship. Who wanted, at forty, to finally settle down.

He braced a hand against the glass, his gaze scanning over the people down below. *Fine.* One person in particular.

Alex hadn't retreated to the Masters' lounge for this purpose, but one glance out the window made him realize that the bird's eye view of the club floor gave him the perfect means of keeping an eye on Blasphemy's newest player. *Not* that he really wanted to be doing that. Problem was, Jamie Fielding was like the bright, warm flame to Alex's cold, lonely heart. And it was fucking hard to look away from the light.

Damnit it all to hell, but when had Alex become so jaded with his life? And how the hell had he not realized just how troubled his state of mind really was?

Down below, Jamie made a loop of the club floor, retracing the steps they'd taken together. He stopped at the backs of already gathered crowds to take in Dominants engaged in various acts with their submissives, and hell if Alex couldn't tell exactly what intrigued Jamie by how long he'd stay or how quickly he'd move on.

The things he lingered at the longest? The first, a punishment scene involving basic bare-handed spanking over a Dom's lap. And the second featured Master Wolf tormenting his exhibitionist Olivia with a multiple forced orgasm scene that seemed to both please and humiliate her, judging by how visibly red her face was, something Alex could make out from all the way up here.

Of all the kink playing out on the floor, his newbie was drawn to the pain and to the humiliation. He fisted his right hand, fighting against the sudden hard desire to feel his palm heat from the repeated impacts against a certain man's ass.

Against Alex's will, his cock hardened.

Which was the moment Alex also realized he'd thought of the man as *his*. And he wasn't. Hell, Jamie didn't even yet belong to himself. *That's* how damn new he was.

"Jesus, McGarry. Get your shit together." Right. Fine. He walked away from the window. Got a drink. Read one of the lifestyle magazines spread out on the coffee table. Went back downstairs with half a mind to just go home.

He was relieved to find that the submissive wasn't at the bar, so he slipped onto an empty bar stool and waited to catch Quinton's eye. He'd let himself have a second drink before he called it a night.

After a few minutes, Quinton did a double take when he saw him sitting there and made his way down the bar. "Hey," he said, his gaze narrowed. "Huh."

"Problem?" Alex asked, chuffing out a laugh.

"Uh, I guess not."

Alex gave him a droll stare. Quinton loved to make a little show of dispensing information. It made him a great freaking storyteller, which was good for the bar or when you were just shooting the shit, but it also made him infuriating when you just wanted him to get to the damn point. Like now. "Say what's on your mind, Master Quinton."

Giving a little shrug, he tilted his head and wiped at the already clean bar top. "I just thought you were with Jamie tonight, that's all. Obviously my mistake."

"Master Kyler asked me to show the kid around, which is what I did. The rest is up to him. Can I get a whiskey, please?"

"Coming right up," Quinton said, reaching for a glass. It didn't take long until he was delivering the drink. "Well, good on the kid. Looks like he's finding his way after all." His gaze landed on something—or someone—over Alex's shoulder.

Alex took a sip of the liquor. Then a deep breath. And then he finally gave in to see what Quinton was getting at.

His gaze landed on Jamie. Who was on his knees at a grouping of seats about thirty feet away. At Master Leo's feet.

Jesus Christ. Alex barely managed to hold back the curse. A boulder lodged itself in his chest, and a wave of what might've been regret—or panic—twisted up his gut. He swallowed hard against an absolutely *brutal* rush of jealousy. He had to give Jamie Fielding this much—his masochistic radar was without question tuned to *sadists.*

Unlike Alex, Master Leo wasn't in it for the pain. He liked the *chase.* The psychological torment that being hunted and stalked could inflict. He was in it for the *mindfuck.* All of which Alex respected.

Except when the man went after what Alex wanted.

What Alex wanted whether he should want it or not.

It took an enormous force of will to turn away from the scene. And then Alex downed the rest of the whiskey in one biting gulp.

Quinton eyeballed him. The fucker was way too observant. Quinton Ross *seemed* easy going and even jovial, but he could read people better than maybe anyone Alex knew. Q leaned in. "You really letting that happen?"

"He's free to play with whomever he chooses," Alex said, his voice a raw scrape. From the alcohol. From the rare overload of emotion. From the *war* raging inside him. Between what he thought was right for him and what he wanted any-fucking-way.

Quinton arched a brow. "He looked at you like the sun rose and set in the palm of your damn hand, Master Alex." *How can you walk away from that?* He didn't voice the question, but Alex heard it. Loud and clear.

And the thing was, Quinton wasn't wrong. Alex could read people, too. And Jamie was an open freaking book.

All the words on his pages might not yet be written in ink, but one thing had been plain as day—Jamie had been interested in Alex.

And Alex had walked away.

He couldn't blame Master Leo for being attracted. Jamie was hot, curious, and eager. And if that wasn't all appealing enough, that striped yellow-and-black ribbon was like a matador's *muleta*—able to attract a sadist's attention and lure them to charge.

Now, Alex had to decide—was he going to allow another Dom to experience Jamie Field's first time playing? Or was he going to claim the submissive for himself? Consequences be damned…

Chapter 6

KNEELING ON THE FLOOR, JAMIE peered up into the Dom's mismatched eyes—one blue, one green. Nervous energy made it hard to sit still as Master Leo asked him questions about his interests—questions that brought Jamie closer and closer to actually doing this. To actually having sex with a near-stranger within a BDSM context.

Jamie *wanted* to do it. He wanted to know if this represented something of what he'd been missing. If this might help explain why he always struggled to connect. If needing these activities explained why he'd messed up so many relationships.

And Master Leo was attractive. Between those unique eyes, and the longish dark blond hair, and the breadth of his shoulders, there was no denying the man's appeal. And there was a look in those eyes that Jamie liked, too. One that said Master Leo could be harsh and intimidating and maybe even scary.

But the problem was that Jamie was making comparisons that made it difficult for him to settle into the what might be happening between them. To give himself over to it. To turn off his thinking mind and just…submit.

Comparisons with Master Alex.

Master Alex who instructed you to find someone to play with. Someone else.

Which, fuck. Maybe he'd read things all wrong, because Jamie had felt like they'd had chemistry. Maybe even the beginnings of a connection. Yet Master Alex hadn't been interested after all. So where did that leave him but to try with someone else? Especially since his holiday travel plans meant he'd only have guaranteed access to the club for half of the two-week provisional membership.

"Have you heard of primal play before, Jamie?" Master Leo asked, peering down at him from the chair where he sat.

"No, Sir," Jamie said, though the sound of it rushed a shiver over Jamie's back.

Master Leo leaned forward so that his knees came around Jamie's upper body, boxing him in, bringing them close. "It's a form of role playing, where I would be the predator, and you would be the prey. Where I would take, and you would let me." He arched a brow over his blue eye. "And where the fucking would be primal, animalistic."

There was no denying that Jamie's body liked *the hell* out of what the Dom described, because his breath caught as blood rushed into his dick. He swallowed hard.

"Is that something you would like to try?"

"Master Leo, I'm truly sorry to interrupt you."

Goosebumps raced over every inch of Jamie's skin. Because that voice had come from right behind where he knelt, and Jamie knew exactly who it belonged to. Jamie's heart was suddenly booming within his chest, so hard that the *whoosh whoosh* of his own pulse inside his ears threatened to drown out everything else.

Except Jamie really wanted to know why, despite his regret, Master Alex *was* interrupting.

"Master Alex," Master Leo said, slowly pulling his gaze away from Jamie, but not at all withdrawing the closeness of his body. "What can I do for you?"

Silence stretched out between the two Dominants, and Jamie ached to turn around and see why Alex wasn't responding, especially as people on nearby seats noticed the quiet confrontation. Finally, his voice rolled out in a low, gravelly tone. "There's no way to say this without causing offense to you, and for that I apologize. But Jamie and I spent time together earlier, and I left him with the erroneous impression that I was done with our conversation. I would like him to know that I erred in creating that impression."

Master Leo didn't move a muscle, but somehow his whole demeanor changed anyway. That was the moment Jamie in fact *saw* just how scary those strange eyes could look. Because the Dom appeared to be *pissed*.

"Please wait, Jamie," Master Leo said, rising. The two Doms stepped away, far enough that Jamie couldn't hear them. But he was absolutely *dying* of curiosity. Because Master Alex *wanted* to spend time with him again. And the only "conversation" they hadn't finished was the one that began with Jamie asking what he was supposed to do next.

Did that mean...? Jesus, what did that mean?

And what the hell was Jamie supposed to do while the two Doms engaged in some sort of a pissing match over him? He was definitely in way over his head here. Even if it was a little bit thrilling.

Forever came and went while Jamie waited, and then Master Leo returned to stand in front of him. Jamie kept his gaze lowered, not sure what to do, and whether the Dom was upset with *him*. So he held his position, remembering what Master Alex had said about the waiting position and how it could represent contrition.

"Look at me, please," Master Leo said. Jamie lifted his gaze. "Master Alex would like a word with you if you're willing?"

Jamie swallowed hard, regretting letting this man down, even if he was pulled more strongly to someone else. He also really respected the way the Dom had phrased his question, instead of more bluntly asking Jamie to make a choice. As if this wasn't already awkward as hell. "I am, Sir."

Master Leo nodded. "Very well. Another time, then. You're dismissed."

"Yes, Sir," he said, rising and feeling more than a little like the ground wasn't quite solid under his feet. Master Leo disappeared into the crowd as Jamie turned, and his gut fell. Because Master Alex was nowhere—

There. At the bar. Looking straight at Jamie like he wanted to make a fucking meal out of him.

"Fuck," Jamie whispered to himself. And then he forced his feet to move. He wasn't sure what he was walking into, but the dark, hot possibility of it made him a little lightheaded. And then he was standing in front of the Dom, heart racing, blood heating, mouth dry. He wasn't sure what to do or say, so he dropped his gaze and waited. There was almost a satisfaction in being able to do that, in being able to hand off that control to someone else.

Master Alex stepped right into his personal space, holding himself just separate from bringing them body to body, and then he gently cupped him by the neck and brought his mouth to Jamie's ear. "I fucked up. And I would like a chance to talk to you. About playing. If you're willing to give it to me."

An exhilarated sweat bloomed over Jamie's whole body and made him suddenly sure he'd give this man almost anything for the reactions he seemed able to wring out of him. With just a touch or a whisper.

But Jamie didn't want to be jerked around, either. Not when this place felt like it could open a door for which he'd maybe been looking forever, and not when his guaranteed time here was so limited. And so Jamie mustered some big brass balls, lifted his gaze, and met the other man's eyes. "I'm new at all this, Sir. But I'm not new at dating or relationships, or hooking up, for that matter. So, are you sure? Because I've kinda had enough of screwing up relationships, and I'm looking for...something here. So if you're not sure, I'd—"

"I'm fucking sure." Master Alex's dark gaze blazed.

Jamie nodded, trying to play it cool even though the rasp of the other man's voice was doing bad, bad things to him, especially as close as they still stood. "Okay."

"Okay." The Dom's grip tightened on Jamie's neck. "So is that a yes?"

"Yes, Si—"

Master Alex kissed him. His mouth hard but his tongue soft where it surged inside Jamie's mouth. Jesus, the man tasted like sin and sex, like he could ruin him and put him back together again. It was a kiss that might've taken Jamie to his knees. A kiss he'd never forget.

Jamie groaned at the goodness of it, at the unexpectedness of it, at how fucking *amazing* it felt to be kissed and held and handled firmly, maybe even a little roughly. At being the recipient of aggressiveness instead of the instigator. His cock was as hard as it'd ever been in his whole life, from a single kiss.

The Dom's grip on him tightened, and he finally hauled their bodies close, allowing Jamie to feel that Master Alex was aroused, too. Jamie's heart tripped into a sprint as he gave into the kiss. It might've lasted for seconds or minutes, but all Jamie knew for sure was that it ended way too soon.

Master Alex pulled away. "That doubt you were feeling, that's on me. I'm sorry. I should've spoken with more care earlier. But I am sure, Jamie."

Did the man think Jamie was capable of speech after that kiss? The world was still fucking spinning around him. "I'm sure, too, Sir," he managed, though his words came out as barely more than a breath.

A single nod. "Then come with me. Somewhere private."

Jamie didn't have to be asked twice. He followed Master Alex through the club again, and it was funny. It was the first time he actually thought about the fact that a *man* had just kissed him in front of a roomful of people. It was a first for him, of course, and therefore new, different. Jamie expected to feel a little self-conscious about that, but was surprised to realize that he didn't care that these people had seen him, nor about what they thought. Not when everyone at the club seemed so open and tolerant. And, more importantly, not when he felt so fucking good about it.

Would Jamie feel so laid back about it in the real world? He didn't know, and Master Alex didn't really give him time to think about it, either. Because just then, they entered the hallway of themed rooms—going about half way before Master Alex paused at a heavy wooden door on the right. The Dom keyed in a code and pushed it open. Soft lighting illuminated the space, and Alex led them inside.

Jamie's heart hammered with anticipation and excitement. The Dom had said they were going to talk, but hopefully they were going to do a helluva lot more than that. Even though Jamie was nervous about…a whole host of other firsts that might mean he'd be experiencing. Still, his travel plans meant that he'd only have maybe six more usable days during his provisional membership at Blasphemy. After that, who knew what might happen. So he wanted to suck the marrow out of every single day he had, and that meant he wasn't just ready to try whatever might be asked of him, he'd decided.

He wanted to experience it *all*.

The room was all dark wide plank floors and stone walls. Heavy, rough-hewn wooden furniture filled the space, including a massive bed and some pieces that weren't regular furniture at all—another Saint Andrew's cross, stocks, different benches and tables with built-in restraints, a cage. It might've been something out of the medieval period, or a medieval torture chamber. Right down to the wall full of hanging implements and toys and the chains suspended from the ceiling. Jesus.

Jamie found the room oddly appealing and definitely intriguing.

"Breathe, Jamie," Master Alex said.

He grinned, and then chuffed out a little laugh. "Yes, Sir."

The hint of a smile played around the Dom's mouth, and then his expression went serious again. "At ease."

It only took a moment for Jamie's brain to respond to what was being asked of him, and he assumed the position.

"Very good." Arms crossed, the man came to stand in front of him. "Master Kyler asked me to introduce you around because I'm a sadist, Jamie. He thought we might be well matched. And he might be right. Are you interested in trying a scene that explores your pain limits?"

It was all Jamie wanted—as long as it came at Master Alex's hands. "Yes, Sir. Very much."

Master Alex nodded, and his gaze dragged over Jamie like a physical caress. "Whatever happens here, I need you to understand that you are ultimately in control. We have safewords to ensure that. You are to use them. *Green* means you're doing good and willing to continue. *Yellow* means you need me to slow down or are approaching your limit. *Red* means you need me to stop immediately. Do you understand?"

Satisfaction rolled through Jamie's gut. He'd read about safewords before coming to Blasphemy, and it was even more reassuring than he'd thought it would be to know he had a safety net. "Yes, thank you, sir."

"Any questions, then? Now's your chance. Speak freely."

Jamie took a moment to think, but his mind was suddenly blank. "Not that I can think of right now, Sir."

A single nod. "Very well. Shoes and shirt off and kneel by the chair. And only speak when I ask you a question."

Swallowing hard, Jamie did as he was told, making a little pile of his belongings by the door. Then he sank to his knees by an armless ornately carved chair, and damn if kneeling didn't ratchet down some of the nervous restlessness he felt. He didn't know what else to do or what might happen, but he knew how to do *this*.

The air was cool against his chest and back, and he found himself hyperaware of his own partial nudity when Master Alex sat before him, still fully clothed. Fuck if the power differential it represented wasn't arousing as hell.

Master Alex heaved a breath and peered down at Jamie with a stern, narrowed gaze. "What am I going to do with you, my little masochist?"

"Anything you want, Sir." The response had come right from the gut. Out of his mouth before he'd even debated whether Alex had meant the question rhetorically.

"Anything I want. Indeed." He tilted his head. "Except you're new to all of this. So I worry—"

"No, *please*," Jamie blurted out, his hands going to Alex's knees. "Don't worry. Don't be easy. I want to try everything. *Do* everything. And I want to do it with you."

A storm erupted across Master Alex's face and settled into those dark eyes, which raked downward to where Jamie still touched him. And then the next thing Jamie knew, Alex launched himself at him, grabbed him by the neck and shoulder, and took him down flat to his back on the floor.

With one hand tight around Jamie's throat and his knees pinning his shoulders and upper body, Master Alex loomed over him, his expression *mean*. "Let me make clear how this works, little boy. I make the decisions. I set the scene. You telling me what to do is called *topping from the bottom*. And I won't have it. Do it again and it'll earn you a red ass you won't be able to sit on for *days*."

Jesus fucking Christ. Yes. *Yes. Fucking yes.*

That was probably *not* the reaction he was supposed to have. And a little voice in the back of his head whispered that there was something seriously wrong with him for feeling sheer exhilaration instead of fear—to say nothing of the way his pulse throbbed in his rock-hard cock. And Jamie certainly didn't want to have made Alex feel disrespected.

But Jesus fucking *yes*.

He swallowed hard, his throat having to work against the tight grip of Master Alex's hand. "I'm sorry, Sir."

Master Alex barreled on. "You're so goddamned sure you can handle this. You don't even know. I'm going to use you and abuse you. I'm going to hurt you. And I'm going to get off on it."

Jamie's cock jerked at the decadent words, and *Jesus* how the dark promise in them reached out to some secret, hidden place inside him. "I don't know…but I want to."

"Why? Why are you here? What do you want out of this? Why the *fuck* do you want the pain I'm capable of causing?" That grip tightened, cutting off more of Jamie's air.

He grimaced and choked. "My…my whole life. I can't—I haven't been able to…*feel*. And I…*want* to finally feel something, Sir. I need it. And I want to please…you," he managed.

Master Alex leaned in, that handsome face so fucking harsh. "Oh, I'll make you feel something, boy. I'll light you up *good*."

God, if Alex was capable of turning his mind and body on so strongly with just two sentences, Jamie almost couldn't imagine what it might feel like for the man to actually make good on the promises. *What if I can't handle it?*

But what if I can?

Jamie whimpered.

Licking his lips, Master Alex nailed him with a stare. "You think you're ready for my cock?"

Jamie groaned. He thought he'd feel more confusion about that question, more hesitation, more worry. But instead, all he felt was a certain brutal terrifying *need*. "Yes, Sir."

"Yes? Really? In here?" He pushed two fingers from his free hand into Jamie's mouth. Not gently. Not slowly. All the way in, until Alex's knuckles hit Jamie's teeth. "In here until you can't breathe?"

Hips surging, Jamie gagged. And he liked that, too. Liked the way Master Alex's eyes flared as he watched himself finger-fuck Jamie's mouth while he struggled to handle it. He attempted to speak around the invasion. To make clear that he was willing to try this. That he was hungry for it. But Jamie's fingers were too ruthless, so he sucked and gagged and took it.

"And how about your ass? You ready for my cock there, too?"

He still couldn't verbalize an answer, so he nodded and pleaded with his eyes and *sucked* on those fingers like they *were* Master Alex's cock.

Jamie knew getting fucked was going to hurt. He'd had one girlfriend who'd been into anal sex, and she'd thought turnabout was fair play. So she'd used toys and her fingers on him, trying to stimulate his prostate. It'd been sexy even though it hadn't always been comfortable, and Jamie hadn't minded the discomfort. Naturally. What he hadn't liked as much was that the woman had been too tentative, too sheepish about exploring him to allow Jamie to really get into it. That obviously wasn't going to be a problem here.

"Maybe I'll take that ass whether it's ready to be taken or not," Master Alex said, withdrawing his hands from Jamie's mouth and his neck.

The loss of the Dom's hard touch nearly left Jamie feeling bereft. "Oh, God, Sir."

A rough tug opened the fly of Jamie's jeans, and then Master Alex was off of him, hauling him up off the floor and then forcing him down again—down over Alex's lap, back on the chair. Jamie's head spun in lust-drunk arousal at the manhandling, even more so when Alex shoved the denim down his thighs, baring Jamie's ass and pinning his cock against the Dom's hard thigh.

"Which will make you scream first, Jamie? My hand against your ass or the strength of your orgasm?"

Smack!

Smack, smack!

Three sharp spanks fell in quick succession against his ass, and all Jamie could do was groan at the goodness of it. Master Alex pinned his back down with his forearm, holding Jamie's upper body firmly in place as his palm rubbed over where he'd just struck.

Then four more spanks fell in a steady rhythm. Hard enough to bring heat rushing into his backside. Hard enough to make Jamie's hips jerk forward, causing him to grind his cock against Master Alex's leg. But not hard enough to truly cause pain. Lighter but still stinging strokes rained down against the backs of Jamie's thighs, making his balls ache and his cock weep.

And then an actual *blow* fell against Jamie's ass, and he howled and writhed as a white-hot flash rocketed through him.

"Yes, let me hear you," Master Alex said, landing another brutal blow on the opposite ass cheek.

The only leverage Jamie had was where his hands and toes touched the floor and where his dick ground against Master Alex. Otherwise, he was suspended inside this rush of painful pleasure, this cloud of sensation that blocked everything else out.

Master Alex rubbed soothing circles against his skin for a moment before two more explosive impacts landed against his ass. Jamie nearly screamed—from the pain, from the pleasure, from the arousal, from finally—for once in his life—feeling *present* in the moment of a sexual situation.

Alex worked at the fly to his own pants. No, not at his fly, at his *belt*. Which he knew for sure when the stiff end of it dragged across Jamie's back. "Now I'm going to push you, boy. Give me your color—tell me where you are."

Color? What? "Oh. Green, Sir. So fucking green."

"Fuck, *yes*," Master Alex rasped. "Then you're going to take this. Take this for me." The Dom bore more weight down on Jamie's back, like he needed additional leverage to do this right. And then the loop of leather struck him straight across the roundest part of both ass cheeks.

Jamie came. Jamie came until he went *blind*. And he screamed and writhed and fought and *came*.

"Four more. Take them."

When the second belting landed, Jamie's cock was still jerking out the last pulses of the orgasm, so all he could do was cry in aroused agony. By the third strike of the leather, tears ran down Jamie's face. By the fourth and fifth, the pain became a soft, white-hot noise that suspended Jamie in time and space.

His ass fucking *hurt*. But the rest of him? Was overwhelmed with sheer joy.

Because there was nothing wrong with him. There was nothing wrong with him at all.

Chapter 7

BREATHING HARD AND SHAKING WITH arousal, Alex eased the two of them down to the floor so that he could hold Jamie in his arms. "Come here, Jamie. Rest on me."

Jamie's sluggish movements revealed that he was still riding the physical and emotional waves of the scene, so Alex helped turn him until he was cradled against his chest. And then Jamie released a breath that resounded with such utter contentment that it reached inside Alex's chest.

Christ. *Christ.* The way Jamie had taken his beating. The way he'd reveled in the pain of it. Alex's twisted sadist heart was flying, because what they'd just shared had been *perfection.*

"Talk to me. Are you okay?" Alex asked, his gaze raking over the relaxed lines of the sub's handsome face and the almost sleepy appearance of his gray eyes. Before, he'd thought Jamie hot. Now, seeing him totally sated because of the pain Alex had given him, he thought him *beautiful.*

"I—I have *never* felt better in my whole life." His voice was little more than a raw scrape, but the emotion behind the words came through crystal fucking clear. "All this time...all this time I thought something was wrong with me. When I just needed this." Those gray eyes slanted up at him. "And you."

Damn if the guy wasn't riding pretty damn close to subspace, a euphoric altered state of mind that some submissives achieved due to the overwhelming rush of endorphins and adrenaline that spiked and receded during intense BDSM scenes. So Alex wasn't going to take the adoration in that steel gaze too much to heart.

"You handled that so perfectly," Alex said, wiping away the wetness of tears or sweat—or both—from Jamie's face. Doing so emphasized the warm heat still filling Alex's palm. He freaking relished it *and* the quiet, calm peace in his mind that he hadn't felt in far too long.

"I did?" When Alex nodded, Jamie smiled. "Thank you." His lids sagged, then snapped back open. "Thank you, *Sir*."

Alex chuckled. "How was the intensity of that for you, Jamie? Did you feel you were nearing your limit?"

He shook his head. "Even though it hurt and I started to feel...shattered, I was green. I was green the whole time."

Jesus. Master Alex brought Jamie's cuffed hand to his mouth and kissed his knuckles. "I think you can switch out the light blue ribbon for the dark."

Jamie's eyes went wide, like Alex had just surprised him with a gift. "Really, Sir?"

See? There was just no questioning the sincerity of Jamie's pleasure, the intensity of his satisfaction, nor how profoundly experiencing his first sadomasochistic scene had affected him. *Still* affected him. And, in turn, Alex, too. Because when had he last seen such unadulterated elation? When had he last witnessed such a pure example of the freeing power of this lifestyle? When had anyone he'd played with recently *found* so much of themselves in a scene?

"Yes, really," Alex said. "This pleases you, I think."

"It does." His gaze went almost shy. "Can I be honest, Sir?"

"I don't want you to ever be anything but."

"I turn thirty in a few weeks, and I'm not sure I've ever fully connected with anyone in a relationship. Tonight, I feel like I'm learning why. I need what you gave me. Which is why, despite only knowing you for a few hours, I feel a connection maybe for the first time ever. So, I don't know, it's just…"

Alex was dying to know what Jamie was trying to say. "What? Just say it however it comes to you."

"You gave me that connection, and I want to give something back to you. So I want to handle everything you have to give."

Oh, man, this kid was dangerous. How many times had Alex recently felt jaded by it all? Jamie had just given him the gift of reminding him what it *could* be. Under the right circumstances. In the right frame of mind.

With the right partner.

Having just that little taste of what this had once meant to him, and what it could maybe be again, Alex wanted *more.*

Because those feelings were heady and exciting and hopeful. But they were also scary as fuck. This could all yet go so many different ways for Jamie. And in even thinking like this, Alex was putting the cart light years ahead of the horse.

Which wasn't smart. Even though Alex knew that, he couldn't stop a part of himself from doing it anyway.

"Are we done, Sir? For tonight, is it over?" Jamie asked.

Alex raked his gaze over the masculine body sprawled against him. Jamie's eyes were clear again, the lust-drenched haze of subspace wearing off. A light brown expanse of hair covered his chest, giving way to the blue and black swirls of a large tattoo that ran up and over Jamie's shoulder and down his arm. His cock lay half-hard against his lower belly, which was still wet here and there from Jamie's orgasm.

Alex *liked* him messy with the proof of his pleasure.

"I don't want to push you too far, too fast, Jamie."

"I understand, Sir," he said, dropping his gaze.

"Are you telling me what you think I want to hear now, little sub?"

A shy smile. "I don't mean to, Sir. I'm trying to respect your wishes and wisdom. It's just, I really do want to try everything. Right now, in this moment. While it feels like this."

"Like what?"

"Perfect."

While it feels perfect. Alex felt that way, too. God, he felt it harder and deeper than he should. Almost desperately, given all that he'd lately been yearning for in his life.

But he didn't want to be selfish, either. And no way in hell did he want to be reckless, or do anything to tarnish the shine of this kid's newfound excitement and enthusiasm.

Jamie swallowed thickly, the sound tortured and parched, a reminder that Alex still had other ways he needed to take care of his submissive. "Do you think you can get up now?"

Frowning, Jamie nodded.

Alex bit back a smile. "Then take off your jeans and kneel for me. I'll get you some water." Jamie did as asked, and Alex didn't miss the spark of hopefulness that lit behind his eyes.

Releasing a long breath, Alex crossed the room, tugged his dress shirt from his slacks, and toed out of his shoes and socks, relishing the cold planks beneath his feet. Next, he went to the small fridge that sat hidden inside the nightstand beside the bed and retrieved two bottles of water. And then he went to a cabinet and grabbed tubes of cream and lube, a package of wet wipes, and a towel before returning to his sub.

His sub.

Careful, McGarry.

The warning was necessary, especially when Alex saw how amazing the man looked kneeling for him. For a long moment, Alex just stared, committing this image to memory. Of the first time Jamie Fielding knelt, entirely naked, at Alex's feet. Seeing this now, he wasn't sure how he'd resisted for even one second claiming Jamie for himself.

He spread the towel in front of Jamie, then handed him a water. "Drink." Alex watched in satisfaction as he quickly swallowed half of it down. Then Alex traded him the wet wipes for the bottle. "Clean my pants of your cum."

Pink filtered into Jamie's cheeks as he wiped at the streaks that marred the dark dress pants. Alex didn't mind the mess, not at all, but he wanted the kid confronted with the reality of what they'd done.

"Sorry, Sir," Jamie whispered, diligently scrubbing at the stain.

Alex grasped Jamie's chin in his fingers and forced him to meet his gaze. "Are you really sorry for this?"

His cheeks went impossibly pinker. "For staining your pants, yes, Sir. For coming on you, no. No, Sir, I find that arousing as fuck."

"Keep talking like that and I'll find a way to punish that mouth." Alex arched a brow, not for a second missing the challenge that flashed through the sub's gaze. "When you're done cleaning me, get on your hands and knees on the towel."

It wasn't long before Jamie moved, giving Alex the chance to do what he'd been *dying* to do. See whether and how his actions had marked Jamie's body, and provide the care that would help ensure those marks weren't permanent.

Alex sucked in a breath at the red stripe that crossed the paleness of Jamie's flesh. "That's fucking beautiful." He knelt and palmed an ass cheek, a deep satisfaction taking root in his gut.

Jamie sucked in a breath, his hips bucking.

"Be still." His fingers traced the stripe his belt had left, extending across one cheek and over the other. "How does it feel?"

"Like an ache that's directly connected to my cock," Jamie said, arousal filtering into his voice again.

Swallowing hard, Alex uncapped the cream, and then he rubbed the marks slowly, reverently, cherishing every moan that spilled from Jamie's throat.

"Makes me so hard to hear you moan and cry and scream, Jamie," Alex murmured, squeezing the cheek just to hear even more of the sub's decadent sounds. He didn't disappoint.

Alex coated his palms with more cream, then grabbed both red cheeks and spread them wide, exposing the ring of Jamie's asshole. *Fuck.* The small pucker of it *begged* to be explored.

His fingers wet with cream, he swiped his thumbs over the hole, coating it with the lotion. Jamie's back arched at the contact, surging blood into Alex's cock. "Aw, you *are* begging for it, aren't you?"

"Yes, Sir," Jamie rasped.

Alex squeezed and swiped, squeezed and swiped, until the tips of both of his thumbs pressed against the ring of muscle. Jesus, he was deliciously tight. Alex was going to enjoy this so fucking much. Getting lube this time, he circled the pad of his thumb against the little asshole, loving the filthy, wet sounds the touch made. And then he pushed inward until his thumb penetrated. Past the fingernail. To the first knuckle.

Jamie threw his head back. "Oh, God, yes."

Alex fucked Jamie with his thumb. Then he pushed deeper and reveled in the new sounds that wrung from the sub's mouth. But he wasn't done pushing him. Not by a long shot. He pushed his other thumb into the forbidding ring of muscle next, doubling the invasion in Jamie's tight hole.

Jamie's *incredibly tight* hole. The sub groaned as Alex's second thumb plumbed deep, as the two together fucked his ass. Alex applied outward pressure against the ring, then a little more as he urged the muscle to widen, loosen, get ready for so much more.

But that ass remained *tight*. *Too* tight? He eased his fingers free, enjoying the groan of disappointment even as his gut latched onto a possibility that was blowing his fucking mind.

"Turn to me and kneel," Alex said, remaining crouched so that they would be eye to eye for this conversation. "When was the last time you had anal sex, Jamie?"

Something flashed behind the sub's eyes, telling him almost everything he needed to know. "About a year ago I had a girlfriend who regularly penetrated me with a dildo."

Alex felt his eyebrows lift as his gut began an uncomfortable tumble. "And?"

"And, uh, that relationship was the only time."

It was like Alex's brain tripped over that revelation, because for a second he couldn't respond. And then the implications of what Jamie just revealed came down on him like an avalanche. "Are you telling me you've never fucked a man?"

"No, Sir," Jamie said. "I've only recently come to realize that I'm attracted to men, too. But when I think about the pain I crave, I feel like I need the strength and size of a man to give it."

He'd never been with a man. Jesus Christ, Jamie Fielding had never been with a man.

And Alex didn't know whether to smash his head against the nearest wall for giving in to the insanity of playing with someone who was *this* inexperienced. Or to get down on his knees and thank whichever god was responsible for giving him the chance to be the one to break Jamie in—in every way he might need breaking. Consequences be damned.

Sure, consequences be damned *for Alex*. That was a risk he could consider taking—even if whether he *should* take it was another question altogether. But Jamie was a fucking virgin. Virgins required initiation, preparation, care.

"Sir?"

Slowly, Alex met the other man's gaze. "Yes, *boy*? Tread carefully."

Jamie nodded, his expression so damn earnest. And not a little determined, too. "Sir, when is it appropriate for a submissive to beg? And how might a submissive do that to show how desperately they desire something, and how much they're willing to debase themselves to have a chance at earning it?"

Alex's heart tripped into a sprint, because that was

possibly the sexiest goddamned question he'd ever been asked in his life. He wanted it stamped on a T-shirt, or mounted on a poster, or maybe even embroidered on a pillow. Jesus. The *mouth* this kid had on him. And the beautifully deviant brain behind it.

"If I were to tell you, just what is it you'd beg *for?*" he asked, his voice like gravel.

Jamie unleashed a shaky breath. "For you to take my virginity. Roughly. Unforgivingly. Maybe even pretending that I don't have a choice in it. And for you to take it tonight. Here. Now."

Chapter 8

JAMIE WAS DONE HOLDING BACK. He was done questioning. He was done feeling like he was on the outside looking in.

Now that Master Alex had demonstrated *exactly* what Jamie required to fully connect with another human being, he needed this to go all the way. More than that, he wanted Alex to be the one to take him there.

So he held his breath, held the Dom's gaze, and held on to the hope that the man would agree.

"You want your first time to be non-consensual role-playing," Master Alex finally said, his voice like it'd been scoured with sandpaper.

The tone of it gave Jamie hope. Because he was affected. Jamie wasn't the only one who needed this, he would've put money on it.

Nodding, Jamie summoned the courage to say what he wanted, while the Dom was still open to hearing it. Even though, *Jesus*, the words on the tip of his tongue were seriously twisted. He let them fly anyway. "I want you to force me, use me, hurt me. To show me what it really means to be taken by a…a—"

"*Say it.*"

"By a sadist."

Master Alex's dark eyes flared, and his expression went a little mean. Jamie's cock hardened, a reaction he couldn't hide when he knelt there naked. The Dom's gaze swept downward and settled on his growing erection, and Jamie felt the directness of that perusal as a physical caress.

Slowly, Alex rose to his full height, and then his expression went absolutely unforgiving. "*Beg.*"

For a moment, Jamie froze at the realization that Master Alex was opening the door. And then he walked through it. "Please, Sir. Please take me. Please use me."

He arched an unimpressed brow and crossed his arms.

What could he do to reach him? To impress him? To convince him? Heart racing in his chest, Jamie thought back to the only guidance he had—the porn videos he'd watched as he'd tried to wrap his brain around what turned him on. And *humiliation* definitely did. So he crawled to Master Alex's feet, knelt again, and peered straight up the man's body.

"Please, Master Alex. I want to be what you need, too. Show me." A dark, hot glare bore down on him, but that wasn't the only thing Jamie saw. Because from under the Dom's dress pants and the wrinkled tail of his shirt, Jamie could make out the jerking movements of Alex's growing erection.

Master Alex arched a brow and stepped backward. "I like it when you beg."

Jamie was desperate for the approval. He stretched his upper body and arms forward until his fingers just grasped Alex's toes. The position ground his knees into the hard floor, but Jamie didn't care. "*Please, Sir.*" When the Dom didn't retreat again, Jamie shifted his whole body forward until he lay prone on the floor, face down, hands caressing and grasping Alex's foot. "Please."

"Spread those fucking legs," Master Alex bit out.

On a groan, Jamie did, feeling exposed and vulnerable. "Please. Please. Let me serve you."

A long, silent tension stretched out, and the next thing Jamie knew was an unforgiving hand clutching his chin and forcing him to arch back so hard that his cock ground into the floor. A pained grunt tore out of him, but Jamie didn't mind, not when his gaze focused on Master Alex crouched before him. He'd removed his shirt and undone his pants, and now he stroked his cock mere inches in front of Jamie's face.

His incredibly *thick* cock. It might've been average in length, but there was absolutely nothing average about its girth. Jamie swallowed hard, a wave of awed terror washing through him. Because he was begging…for that baseball bat to penetrate him.

"You beg so pretty, boy. I'm going to give you what you think you want." The smile that crawled up Master Alex's face was pure evil in the night.

Jamie's whole body flashed hot.

Alex lazily stroked that fat cock as he spoke, still forcing Jamie to hold the uncomfortable position. "You remember your safe words?"

"Yes, Sir."

"Tell me."

Jamie released a shaky breath. "Green for good. Yellow for slow down. Red for stop."

A single nod. "You understand that we are *role-playing*. If you say your safeword, I will stop immediately. But saying things like *no* or *stop* or *you're hurting me* won't make me stop. In fact, I just might do it harder if you let me know you're in pain. So you must use your safewords if I push you too hard toward a limit."

Jamie loved that he took the time to make that clear. "Yes, Sir."

"I will wear a condom when I penetrate you, because even though I want to hurt you, I need you to know that I will always keep you safe." One eyebrow arched in a dark slash.

Jamie was naked. Prone. Held in a way that made his back and cock ache. And yet those words still rushed affection through his whole body. Affection for this man. "Thank you, Sir."

"Then I want you in the bed. Pretend to be asleep, Jamie. That's the set-up. Everything else is fair game."

Jamie's pulse spiked in aroused anticipation. This was *exactly* what he'd hoped for. "I understand, Sir."

"Then, go. I'm no longer Master Alex to you. And you're no longer Jamie. We're strangers, and I'm about to invade your world."

As Jamie crossed to the big bed and drew back the covers, Master Alex disappeared through a door near the wall of toys.

"Holy fuck," he whispered to himself, half sure he must be dreaming as he slipped between the cool sheets. It seemed so impossible that he'd found all this so suddenly. He'd come home from work on Friday night and been Jamie Fielding, straight-laced attorney and boyfriend of Liz Stein. And now he lay here on Monday night, naked in a strange bed in a sex club, about to be violated by a sadist man intent on hurting him—which was exactly what he'd begged for and precisely what he'd been searching for. For so very long.

The lights dimmed, though they remained high enough

that he could still see. But it helped create the *illusion*. And it was just one more thing that helped Jamie understand that a lot about the fulfillment that BDSM had to offer stemmed from the psychological aspects of the power dynamic and the role playing and even submission, itself.

So he gave himself over to the illusion, too. He stretched out in his favorite position, one leg straight out and the other drawn up so that he lay partly on his side and partly on his stomach. And then he closed his eyes. For a few moments, his ears attempted to compensate for the loss of vision, until he was almost straining for the sounds that might reveal Master Alex's nearness. But then Jamie forced himself to count his breaths—in for two and out for two. In for two, out for two. Until, finally, his brain tuned out and his body relaxed and his mind drifted for long minutes.

A door creaked. Near silent footsteps padded upon the floor. Fabric rustled. Little noises Jamie couldn't decipher.

The mattress depressed.

Jamie's gut went on an insane loop-the-loop.

The covers dragged downward, baring his back. Jamie shifted onto his left side, determined to feign sleep until something about Alex's—*no*, the *intruder's*—actions was disruptive enough that it might've awakened him for real.

Something gently looped around his right wrist. Slowly, his arm was lifted and repositioned to rest on his hip. And then behind, to the small of his back.

Jamie frowned, and his eyes eased open, blinking into the dimness.

Someone loomed over him—

Gasping, Jamie wrenched into a sitting position. "What the fuck?"

But the masked intruder was on him before he'd even finished uttering the question, forcing him down, then onto his stomach. Jamie fought and twisted and wrestled and cursed.

"Get the fuck off me! Who the fuck are you?"

A knee planted itself in the center of Jamie's back, then the man made a play for his other wrist, but Jamie bucked hard, nearly throwing him off balance. If he could just get off the bed and run…

He nearly threw himself toward the edge, but the man's whole weight came down on top of him and his arm wound round his throat. "Keep fighting and I'll cut you," came a terrifying voice in his ear. Something sharp pressed against his neck just below his jaw.

"Fuck you," Jamie spat, even as blood surged into his cock. The blade pressed hard enough to shoot Jamie's pulse into a staccato beat, and he groaned.

"We can do this the easy way or the hard way. I'm happy to make you bleed for me."

Jamie held still. "What do you want, man? Money? My wallet's on the table."

The sharpness shifted to the back of Jamie's neck as the man pushed onto his knees. "Not money."

"What then?" Jamie turned his head.

"Don't fucking move."

Suddenly, something looped around his left hand, something hard and unyielding. And then the restraints on his hands were cinched together, securing his wrists at the small of his back. The man grasped Jamie by the arm and flipped him over, forcing him to rest on the uncomfortable combination of his pinned arms and still-healing shoulder tattoo. But Jamie barely had time to react to that before the man straddled Jamie's thighs and applied a third restraint—another zip tie, as it turned out—around the base of Jamie's ball sack.

The tight, almost cutting squeeze made him yell and

buck. He peered up at his tormenter. Shirtless. Black dress pants undone at the waist. Black medical gloves on his hands. Black mask with openings that revealed only his sneering mouth and dark, glaring eyes.

"You going to cooperate now?" He held up the pocket knife, turning it so the dim light glinted off the blade. "Or can I put this away."

"Fuck you, asshole."

The man folded and pocketed the knife, and then he lithely dismounted him and the bed in one fluid movement. Jamie tracked his motions and watched him drop his pants to the floor. And Jesus the man was all lean muscle. Not ripped, but hard looking. A wall of masculinity. Jamie had been so mesmerized by his admiration that he realized he wasn't sure what Alex was planning until he stepped to the edge of the bed and hauled Jamie so that his head hung backward off the mattress.

"Time to give that smart mouth what it really needs," his attacker gritted out, taking his beast of a cock in hand. The man squeezed Jamie's jaw. Hard. "Open."

"No, man." Jamie clamped his mouth shut and twisted and turned as much as he could.

"*Open.*" He pinched Jamie's nose, making his mouth pop open to gasp down a breath.

Cock suddenly filled Jamie's mouth. Hot. Heavy. Thick. Overwhelming. Jamie moaned at the decadence of the sensation, at the strain in his jaw from trying to accept the invasion, at how the position restricted Jamie's sight to Alex's full ball sack. At having another man's cock inside him for the first time in his life.

"Bite me and I'll hurt you worse," the man spat, pinching and twisting both of Jamie's nipples. He bucked and moaned, his mouth over full. And, God, his own cock was throbbing so hard that Jamie would've given anything to have been able to take it in hand and give it just one good stroke. A desire that made him hyperaware of the cutting restriction around his scrotum.

Jamie was absolutely drowning in Alex. His musky, masculine scent. The too-big mouthful of his cock. His rough touch.

"You can do better than that," Alex growled, shoving his hips forward. "Take it all."

Choking and gasping, instinct had Jamie trying to rear or turn away, but the position meant he couldn't move far.

"No!" Alex said, bringing both gloved hands down against the muscles of his pecs. Fire raced across his skin from the impact. "Take it all in your mouth or you won't get it anywhere else."

"Please," he whimpered, no longer sure if he was asking the intruder to stop or Alex to continue. Fantasy and reality tumbled and melded until Jamie didn't know what was up or down. He only knew Alex. *Only Alex.*

"Take my cock, boy." The fat head pressed into Jamie's mouth again and surged inward. "Let it fill that pretty mouth. Let it hurt for me."

One hard, gloved hand planted itself in the middle of Jamie's chest, and the other grasped the back of Jamie's head. And then Master Alex face-fucked Jamie without the slightest bit of mercy.

His hips thrust. Alex's hand forced Jamie's head to meet those thrusts halfway. And that big cock closed off the back of his throat again and again. Jamie gagged and gasped and moaned. Tears leaked from the corners of his eyes and saliva smeared onto his cheeks. It was dirty and debasing and suffocating. His neck ached and his jaw ached and his balls ached from the arousal gathering behind the restriction of the zip tie.

"Yes, *yes*," Alex rasped, his hips picking up speed, his strokes going deeper. "Now take it all." With both hands grasping the back of Jamie's head, the Dom forced him to impale his throat on the impossibly fat head of that cock. Jamie took him so deep that Alex's heavy ball sack covered his face. A strangled groan tried to rip from Jamie's mouth, and the burn of air deprivation kindled in his chest. "Hold it." Jamie's sounds became more desperate, and tendrils of real fear twined with the lust. "*Fucking hold it.*"

But he couldn't, and his body wouldn't be denied. His shoulders wrenched and his hips bucked and he unleashed a strangled scream.

"Yes," Alex roared, stepping clear.

Jamie's breathing sawed in and out of him as sweet oxygen returned. He was overwhelmed and drowning in sensation and needed friction against his cock so fucking bad that he could've cried.

Bringing their faces close, Alex said, "Look how pretty you are." He licked at the corner of Jamie's eye, tasting his tears. How could something be so affectionate and so twisted at the same time?

"Are you…are you done with me yet?" Jamie managed, struggling to crawl back into his character's skin. "Just go."

"No, I'm not going to be done with you for a long, long time." Alex smacked his face. "I think I could get addicted to these sweet tears." He smacked him again, little stinging humiliations.

Then Alex stepped away and rounded the bottom of the bed in the dimness. Jamie wasn't sure where he'd gone until hands grasped his ankles and tugged him so that his legs hung off the opposite side of the mattress.

"Somebody is enjoying this I see." Alex squirted lube

onto his glove, then roughly grabbed and pumped Jamie's erect cock. After yearning for the friction, Jamie nearly screamed. The tight grip worked his length so damn good and hard and fast that Jamie's orgasm was suddenly barreling down his spine.

Painful pressure built up into his balls until Jamie was groaning. "Gonna come!"

Alex removed his hand and then smacked his dick. Hard. "Not yet, boy."

"No!" Jamie cried, strung tighter than he'd ever been in his whole life.

Paying him no mind, Alex rolled him enough to use a pair of cutters to remove the zip ties from Jamie's wrists. Then he ripped off his mask and threw it to the floor. The quick movement disheveled his brown hair, giving the Dom a sexed-up look that was a total stunner.

Taking his time, Alex generously lubed himself, and then he lifted Jamie's legs and spread them wide, gifting Jamie's ass hole with the same treatment.

"Good thing you decided to cooperate with me," Alex said with a sneer. "I would've happily taken you dry."

Jamie moaned as first two, then three wet gloved fingers fucked and stretched his ass. "Thank you, Master," he whimpered, head absolutely spinning.

Alex's eyes blazed. "Enough." He yanked his fingers free. "Look at my face. And know whose cock that ass belongs to."

Their gazes collided. Alex pushed one of Jamie's legs to his chest, holding him open. And then he guided his cock into Jamie's virgin ass.

"*Aaah!*" Jamie groaned, the burn unimaginable. "You're too fucking big," he gritted out as what felt like a pole invaded his ass.

"You will take this for me," Alex growled. "You will

let my cock tear you up. And you will scream my name while you come."

Torn between dizzying lust and abject terror, Jamie howled. His body writhed. His ass was white-hot fire.

Alex's cock shoved past the tight ring of muscle at the entrance to Jamie's rectum, and Jamie saw *stars*. And right behind the exploding burn was the heaviest, most intense sensation of fullness he'd ever before felt. "Oh, *fuck*. Oh fuck oh fuck."

"Yes, take it. This dirty little hole needs some training, doesn't it?"

Jamie was too overwhelmed to answer. He reached for his cock, hoping his hand might provide something good to even out the pain.

But Alex smacked his hand away. "That's *my* fucking cock, boy. But you want some attention? I'll give it some attention." Alex reached for something laying on the bed, then held up a long-handled crop with a small leather head—which he immediately used to tap at Jamie's cock and balls.

Jamie screamed and bucked, unintentionally impaling himself deeper onto Alex's massive pole. Awash in a sea of pain, Jamie finally could do nothing except give himself over to it. Entirely. Utterly. And, God help him, gratefully.

Alex saw it the moment Jamie gave into the pain. His eyelids went heavy. His hands fell lazily to the bed. And his asshole relaxed, just a little.

It was beautiful fucking submission. And it made Alex want to crawl inside this man until they could never be separated again.

Which was when Alex let himself off the hook. His

hips absolutely pistoned, his cock going deeper and deeper and deeper until Jamie's tight little ass got close to swallowing him all. The *smack* of colliding, sweat-covered skin rang out in the room in a rhythm against which Alex's harsh breaths and Jamie's moans and cries and murmured pleas played.

And then Alex twisted them both a little higher by smacking Jamie with the crop. Against his nipple, his thigh, his hip. Against his weeping, half-erect cock and those tight, red balls. Each impact hit Alex like a jolt of adrenaline in his veins, sending him higher and higher.

"*Pleasepleaseplease*," Jamie cried, his face a mask of shattered pleasure so pure that Alex half believed he could live without food or water or air if only he could see this man wear that expression every goddamned day.

"Taking my cock, Jamie. Taking it so good." He couldn't hold back the praise. Because this man was fucking special. Brave and adventurous, real and guileless. So filled with life and power. And restoring those inside Alex, too. A true masochist to Alex's demanding sadist.

"It hurts, Master," Jamie babbled. "It hurts so bad and so good and I don't...I can't..."

"Sshh," Alex said, more than a little overwhelmed by how much he reveled in the sub's slip. *Master*, as if Alex owned him, versus *Master Alex*, a sign of respect due his status as one of Blasphemy's Master Dominants. He lowered his weight to Jamie's chest, driving his cock in to that protesting hole even deeper. With one hand, he gripped Jamie's shoulder, gaining leverage to grind and hump himself against the other man. And with the other, he cupped the back of Jamie's head and brought them face to face. "Tell me it hurts again."

"It hurts," Jamie rasped, his eyes almost silver from the sea of glassy tears.

"Tell me you love it."

"I do. I love it. I do." His voice cracked.

Possessiveness flooded through Alex like a drug—a drug he'd never taken before. "Tell me who hurts you so good."

"You, Master Alex. You hurt me so good."

Alex kissed him then, wanting to taste the salt of tears and sweat that slicked the other man's lips. He sipped and licked and sucked at Jamie's mouth, enjoying exploring him with his lips and tongue and teeth while his cock was shoved deep.

And then Jamie buried his hands in Alex's hair and kissed him right back.

It was just a kiss. It was just a goddamned kiss.

But something inside of Alex shifted when the other man claimed him that way. Maybe Jamie didn't mean anything by it. Maybe Alex was too physically and emotionally raw to be rational. But Jamie Fielding did *not* feel like just another submissive, just another play partner. And it didn't seem to matter one fucking bit to his mind, his body, or his heart that he could still count the hours he'd known the man on one hand.

That emotional whirlwind shoved Alex's body hard toward release, and with regret he broke the kiss and stood up once again. Taking Jamie's cock in his gloved hand, he jacked him in time with the snapping swings of his own hips.

"Come, Jamie. Show me how much you love my pain. *Come.*"

The sub groaned and cried and fucked his fist as much as Alex's cock would let him. "Alexalexalex!" he screamed. "Fucking God, Alex!"

Alex felt the orgasm before he saw the evidence of it, because Jamie went brutally tight inside. It only took the first massive eruption of cum to set off Alex's orgasm. He pulled out, stripped the condom from his cock, and shot his load over Jamie's cock and balls, even as Jamie was still coming, too.

Alex's head spun. His equilibrium was for shit. And his legs were like fucking Jell-o.

But none of the ways this scene, this *whole night*, had shattered him physically compared to the power of the emotional earthquake rumbling inside him.

On either side of his hips, Jamie's thighs shook. His whole body trembled. "Hold on, I've got you. I need to take the zip tie off first."

In answer, Jamie's teeth chattered.

Alex used the cutters to carefully remove the plastic from around Jamie's genitals, then pushed the pile of toys to the side and stripped off the gloves.

When he crawled into the bed, he pulled Jamie in so they were chest to chest, and wrapped him in a blanket. Alex rested his head on a pillow and studied the other man, whose head fell heavily on his biceps. And he had thoughts that felt fucking amazing to have, and were also quite possibly reckless beyond all imagining.

Thoughts of tomorrow and tomorrow and tomorrow.

"Are you okay?" Alex asked quietly.

"Yes," Jamie said. He licked his lips, his gaze not quite tracking. "I…I feel…I can't…"

Alex stroked his cheek. "It's called subspace, little one. It's proof of how beautifully you submitted and how high you flew. Give in to it and sleep. I'll be right here when you wake up."

Chapter 9

COME BACK TOMORROW NIGHT.

Jamie had heard that four times this week. And he wasn't sure whether it was Master Alex's beautifully vicious cock, the Dom's expertise at dispensing pain, or the obvious affection winding between the two of them that had kept Jamie riding the highest of highs all damn week.

Come back tomorrow night.

The first time Master Alex had said it was when Jamie had woken up sleeping on him after their first penetration scene. It had been three o'clock in the morning, long after the club had closed, by the time Jamie finally emerged from the sex coma. He'd even called it that and made Master Alex laugh.

Jamie had obviously been thunder struck by the sex, by their compatibility, by what Alex was able to make him feel—at long last. But as they'd laid together talking that night, Jamie found himself admiring his sense of humor, the way he kept touching and petting him, and how he kept checking to make sure Jamie was okay.

They'd only gotten out of bed at six because they both

had to go to work. And as Alex led him out of the club's staff entrance to a private courtyard around the back of the church, Jamie learned that Alex was a psychiatrist and owned a practice. He'd then driven Jamie from the Masters' private lot the two blocks around to where he'd left his own car, where they sat talking for another half hour until Jamie was sure he was going to be late. And he hadn't really cared if he was. It'd felt like they couldn't get enough of asking each other questions and learning the million mundane things that made up a life—things that were interesting when it was the life of someone about whom you cared.

By the time Jamie made it to work at eight forty-five Tuesday morning, he felt like he'd been away on vacation. For days. Or weeks. And that he'd come back a whole new man.

And he'd been only too eager to accept Master Alex's invitation to come back again that night—when the Dom introduced him to the painful pleasure of being chained and flogged while his cock was tormented with a tight, vibrating silicone sleeve. Jamie's skin had nearly glowed at the end of that scene, though even that hadn't compared to how it felt to have the Dom praise him and hold him and ask him, again, *come back tomorrow night.*

Wednesday night had given him what Master Alex had denied him the night before—another ride on the man's terrifying cock. But first the Dom insisted that his asshole needed *training*, which involved fucking Jamie with an enormous black dildo, nearly as scary in girth as it was in length. Just when Jamie had been certain that he couldn't handle any more of the toy's twelve inches, Master Alex had hauled him back against his chest, forcing him to sit all the way down on it until he'd taken it all. Then he'd earned his Master's cock, two massive orgasms, and his most intense sex coma yet. And when he'd awakened, those cherished words, *come back tomorrow night.*

Master Alex had been especially sadistic on Thursday night. He'd made Jamie kneel and then chained his wrists above him, and then the Dom had forced Jamie up just enough to lay beneath his spread thighs. It had been sexy as hell to be the one pinning Alex down until he'd revealed how the pain would come into their play—Jamie would be forced to cause his own pain by fucking himself on the monster cock below him. At first, Jamie thought there might be some advantage in that. But Master Alex ensured that Jamie would have no real control by using a remote to tighten and slacken the wrist chains suspending him and by shocking him with some sort of electrical wand. And between the surprise adjustments of the chains, the aching strain that settled into his shoulders, and the burning bites of the electroshock, Jamie finally had to submit, once again, to the inevitability of being utterly conquered by Master Alex's cock.

That night had lasted until the morning just like their first one had. It'd been another night filled with conversation that was as fulfilling as the sex. They talked about their families and jobs, how Alex had realized he was a sadist, and likes and dislikes, leading Jamie to realize that they had way more in common than their sexual deviance. They were both bisexual and had struggled to find a lasting relationship with either women or men. They both spent too much time working and worried that they weren't good at creating relationships with other people. Neither had as many close friends as they wished. They both liked to read and to run and to be out on the water in the summer. And they both wanted to see each other again on Friday night.

Tonight.

And so here Jamie was, back at Blasphemy for the fifth night in a row, to see a man who had turned his whole world upside down. And who threatened to make Jamie love him with every moment they spent together.

Some people might've thought it was way too soon to be thinking in terms of emotions. And maybe it was. But all the hours they'd spent together and, even more importantly, all the intimacy they'd shared, made their time feel like the equivalent of weeks' worth of dates. Maybe even more than that.

Anyway, what did Jamie know about love? Since he'd never fallen into it before. At the very least, Jamie had never felt this desperate euphoric *need* for another person before. The kind that made it a torment to leave someone's presence. The kind that made you want to orient your whole day around just the chance to talk to a person. The kind that made you read the same damn patent application ten times over because your mind refused to think of anything else besides *him*.

Standing in front of his locker at Blasphemy, Jamie let out a low curse. "Oh, fuck me." Who was he kidding? Alex didn't threaten to make Jamie love him. Alex had *already* conquered his heart as well as his body.

What he was supposed to do with that revelation, Jamie didn't know. And luckily he had something else to think about. Because he found a card atop a small box in his locker.

Jamie,

Insert this. You know where. And then put on only your jeans and meet me at the bar.

—A

Inside the box was a four-inch anal vibrator with an attached cock ring. A slow grin crawled up his face as he examined it, but he couldn't find a way to turn it on. Using some lube on the bathroom counter, Jamie made quick work of inserting it, and then he stepped back into his jeans. And hell if trying to walk around with something inserted in your ass didn't make you feel it with every single step. Heading out of the locker room, Jamie carried the Christmas gift he'd brought. The big day wasn't for another three days, but Jamie was flying to California in the morning to spend a week-long holiday visit with his parents.

A week ago, Jamie had been glad to be getting out of Baltimore. Now, leaving sat like a rock in his gut.

God, he had it really freaking bad, didn't he?

A few minutes later, he was making his way through the crowded club toward the bar. The vibe was festive and a little frenetic, and it sent a shiver of arousal through Jamie's blood. He couldn't find a seat at the big marble-and-iron counter that formed the bar, so he squeezed in at one end, giving himself a decent one-eighty view of a wide section of the floor that would hopefully allow Master Alex to spot him.

"Can I get you something?" a deep voice asked from behind him.

Jamie turned and looked into the mismatched eyes of Master Leo. "Oh, hello, Sir. No, thank you. I'm waiting for someone."

"For Master Alex," he said.

Ah, holy awkward. "Yes, Sir."

"Good for him, then." He winked. "Let me know if you change your mind."

"I will, Sir," Jamie said, meaning about a drink. But then it occurred to him that maybe the Dom had meant it in some other way.

His thoughts were all tangled around that axle when a hand slid around his waist. "Were you waiting long?"

Jamie grinned. "Not at all, Master Alex. Hello."

"Hello." The Dom murmured the greeting against his lips before kissing him deeply, lingeringly. And then he bit on Jamie's bottom lip, just a little stinging nip. But it made Jamie hot for the man. "Did you find my present?"

"Wearing it now, Sir."

Approval banked heat in those dark eyes. "Good boy. Come with me," he said, entangling their fingers. "I'd like us to hang out with some people for a bit, and they saved us seats."

"Yes, Sir," Jamie said, willing to follow the man pretty much anywhere. Following had another benefit—it gave him the opportunity to really look his fill at this man who'd planted his flag in Jamie, claiming pretty much everything he had to give. And Alex, Alex managed to be both harshly masculine and classy and refined all at once. He wore what Jamie had come to think of as his club gear—the black slacks and black-button down combo with the sleeves cuffed that now made Jamie's mouth water like a fucking Pavlovian response.

Master Alex stopped short just before they reached the grouping of couches. "Our scene begins now, Jamie. Do you understand?"

His pulse kicked up under his skin. "Yes, Sir."

"You will kneel at my feet. And no speaking unless I ask you a question or direct you to."

Jamie nodded and goosebumps rushed over his skin. This was the first time Master Alex had ever called something they'd done in the public spaces of the club a *scene.* And without yet knowing what his Dom was going to require of him, Jamie felt self-conscious and nervous.

And way more excited.

Damn Master Alex for knowing just how much humiliation turned him on. And damn his own twisted brain. Not that he really minded. Jamie far preferred understanding and accepting his own deviance than being a stranger to himself who couldn't connect with others. But still, damn his fucking awesome sadist of a Dom.

Master Alex led them to the couches and introduced everyone. Masters Kyler and Quinton and their subs, Mia and Cass, Jamie had already met. Master Griffin and his submissive, Kenna, were new but familiar to him—they were the couple he'd watched do the bondage demonstration on his first night.

"Everyone this is Jamie Fielding. Jamie, say hello," Master Alex instructed.

Standing a half step behind his Dom, Jamie gave a wave. "Hello, Sirs. Ladies."

Master Alex sat in a leather wingback chair and Jamie knelt, his knees touching the man's shoe. He placed his gift on the floor, and then assumed the waiting position, gaze down. It was an interesting challenge to both submit to this position and remain situationally aware and alert in case Master Alex called for him, especially when he wasn't involved in the others' conversation. But it became easier when Alex gifted him with little caresses and touches, stroking his hair, massaging his neck, tracing the lines of his tattoos with a single dragging finger. Centering Jamie with the evidence of his attention.

A sensation. No, a *vibration*. From deep inside his ass.

Jamie bit back a moan at the pressure against his prostate.

"Look at me," came Master Alex's voice.

He did, and aw, man, the blatant lust in those dark eyes rushed heat over Jamie's skin. The vibration increased, and his cock hardened, tormented by the tight circle of the toy's ring.

"What do you want?" the Dom asked, spreading his thighs.

Jamie didn't have to think about this. "To do whatever would please you, Master Alex." He wasn't just saying that either. Not only had he learned that submitting to the sadist's torture always rewarded him with pleasure in the long run, but all week Jamie had found that he was happiest when he'd pleased or satisfied Alex, or when he received the Dom's praise.

Now he *craved* that.

"Move between my knees and take out my cock."

Jamie's stomach went for a loop, like he'd just crested the highest hill on a tall roller coaster. This *was* different, engaging in such an intimate act in front of others.

"Where is your mind right now, boy? On me."

On Alex. Only Alex. Nodding, Jamie shifted positions and unzipped Alex's pants. He wore nothing underneath, allowing that big cock to spill out into his hand. And there was nothing like this fat dick to chase the rest of the world away.

Master Alex nailed him with a stare that brooked no argument. "Make me come with your mouth."

Knowing what the Dom liked, Jamie didn't hesitate and he didn't hold back. He held the thick pole in one hand, spit on the wide head, and opened his mouth as he sucked him in. On some level, Jamie felt hundreds of eyes watching him, and it was possible a blush was blooming across every inch of his skin. But Alex's size didn't give him the luxury of lax concentration, and so he put everything into taking the cock deep, deep, deeper.

Alex stroked his shoulders, his hair, his hand. He ratcheted up the vibrator until Jamie was all but humping the front of the chair. And then, out of nowhere, he roughly grabbed the back of his head and forced him all the way down.

Jamie didn't want to fight him. Didn't want to struggle. Didn't want to fail to make him proud. Not in front of all these people. So he moaned and he gagged and he accepted the burn of the deprivation of air. But what he didn't do was fight.

For just a moment, Master Alex let him up. Air sawed into Jamie's lungs, and then the Dom bit out, "Again."

The blow job went on that way for long delirious minutes. Oxygen-stealing deep throating interspersed with brief windows of air and control. Until tears streamed down Jamie's face and his cock needed to explode.

"I'm going to give you my cum, Jamie, and you're going to swallow every fucking drop." Mouth too full to speak, Jamie nodded. And Alex rewarded him with a few smacks against his tear-streaked face. And then Master Alex groaned, too. "Get ready. Get ready to take it. Show me what a slut you are for my cum."

On an up-stroke, the first hot jet of the orgasm hit the back of Jamie's throat. He'd blown Master Alex several times, but he'd only drank down his load once before. He tried to swallow as fast as he could, but his Dom fucked his face through the repeated pulsing of his release and some spilled out onto Master Alex's cock.

The Dom pulled him off his erection and shook his head. "I said every drop. Clean me with your tongue." Between knowing he hadn't done what his Master had required and the word *slut* still ringing in his ears, heat roared into Jamie's face. But he licked up what he'd spilled, the taste salty and sweet. "Better," Master Alex said in a low voice.

He peered up at the man, gratitude on the tip of his

tongue, but he wasn't supposed to speak.

Alex tucked himself away and closed his pants, then gave a single nod like he knew what Jamie wanted. Of course he did. He always seemed to. "Thank me."

"Yes, Sir. Thank you, Sir."

"Your reward." The vibrations inside him spiked so hard Jamie yelped. Alex chuckled. "Relax now," he said, gently pushing Jamie's head to rest on his still-spread thighs and stroking his hand over his hair. Jamie no longer knew who was around them or who might be paying them any mind, but he didn't care. He couldn't care. And he couldn't relax either.

Because the vibrator was absolutely brutalizing Jamie's prostate and calling forth what was sure to be a huge orgasm. He fought against it and he moaned and shifted, but it was impossible to still his hips. One hand fisted in the fabric of Alex's pants leg. And still the Dom said nothing.

Jamie was going to come. He was going to fucking come. His moans became alarmed cries and he slanted his gaze upward. Master Alex's dark eyes were trained on Jamie's face. He knew what was about to happen.

Alex mouthed a single word. *Come.*

The orgasm barreled down Jamie's spine and nailed him in the lower back and then it exploded out the front of his cock inside his jeans. He cried out, his head grinding into the muscle of the man's thigh.

But the vibrations didn't stop. And Master Alex didn't stop watching Jamie's face.

Jamie shook his head, silently pleading, silently praying. He couldn't tolerate the intensity of the assault. He couldn't come again. He couldn't stay quiet when he was so fucking sensitive.

"You're going to come again, Jamie," Master Alex said.

"You're going to give me your release."

And he was right. Jamie came again in a brutally hard orgasm. And then he screamed through a third time and a fourth. He hadn't even known his body was capable of such a thing. Nor that an orgasm could feel so good and so painfully bad at the same time.

When the toy finally turned off, Jamie lay absolutely limp in Master Alex's lap.

The Dom pressed a single kiss atop his head.

And only his utter exhaustion kept Jamie from giving voice to the love he felt for the other man.

Chapter 10

"WELCOME TO THE MASTER'S LOUNGE," Alex said, guiding Jamie into the private space. The Masters did occasionally bring subs here, though usually that was reserved for those in committed or collared relationships. But Alex hadn't thought twice about bringing Jamie, not when his own actions had trashed the man's clothing.

He owed Jamie a shower, and since he wanted to take it with him, they'd come here.

"Thank you, Sir," Jamie said, peering around, his expression solemn like he understood that coming here was special. He went to the big window. "What an incredible view. You can really see the beauty of the building from up here."

"Indeed," Alex said, taking the other man in. Just observing and watching. Because he couldn't fucking get enough.

Jamie caught him looking, and Alex let him, continuing the blatant stare until Jamie's cheeks pinked and he chuckled. "Is anything wrong, Sir?"

"Fuck, no."

The sub ducked his chin and grinned, which made Alex realize he still carried a square wrapped box in his hand.

"What's that?" he asked.

Now the kid's smile turned a little shy. "It's just something small. For you. Merry Christmas."

"That was very thoughtful of you," Alex said, opening the paper and then the carton underneath. He pulled out a black coffee mug that said, *I think the phrase you're searching for is Yes, Master.* Alex chuckled at the humor of it, even as that phrase played with things in his chest. *Yes, Master.* He should've corrected Jamie when he'd said it, but he liked hearing it too fucking much to correct him. And didn't *that* say something. "This might become my new favorite saying."

Grinning, Jamie nodded. "There's something inside, too."

Pulling out the tissue paper inside the mug, Alex could feel the weight of something solid wrapped inside. A slim titanium identification bracelet spilled into his palm with his initials engraved into the front in a bold, classic lettering.

A M M

Alexander Michael McGarry.

The piece was beautiful, tasteful, refined. And it moved Alex to a surprising degree. Maybe because he'd been debating trading out Jamie's white cuff to red, and marking him as attached. But Alex had hesitated. Fuck, he'd hesitated because he wasn't nearly as fearless as the younger man before him. But now he knew he should've done it. Now everything inside him was screaming *attached* so loud he could no longer ignore it. "How did you learn my middle initial?" he managed to ask around the emotion lodged in his chest.

"Master Kyler." He cleared his throat and said more quietly. "Turn it over."

Alex flipped the bracelet and found more engraving on the inside.

You are my weakness.

You are my strength.

"Jesus, Jamie," he said, completely overwhelmed. "I fucking love it." Alex couldn't keep his distance any longer. He got right up in Jamie's space and cupped his hands around Jamie's face. And then he kissed him like he was the air Alex needed to breathe. "I will cherish this."

They stood with their foreheads touching. "I just wanted you to know that, no matter what else happens, I am who I am because of everything you've given me."

"Aw, my sweet boy. You were strong before you ever walked into this place. Never forget that." And then Alex just couldn't stop with the praise, not when the man had so lit him up inside. "You did so good tonight. Was it hard, in front of people?"

"A little. I'm not used to being so open. But more than that, I didn't want to do anything to embarrass you."

Alex appreciated the sentiment, but he shook his head. "You're going to make mistakes. Hell, so am I. You've come an incredibly long way in a short amount of time, Jamie. I'm proud of you." Alex kissed him again, unable to get enough of the man's touch and taste and service.

And even more than being proud, Alex was *awed* by Jamie Fielding. The man had been nothing but fearless all week. Fearless in trying so many new things, in his commitment to learning more about himself, in accepting Alex's sadism, and in being willing to show exactly how much it meant to him.

With each passing day, Alex had allowed himself to hope a little more, a little stronger, that he and Jamie could be about more than sex. They had conversations late into the night, the kind he hadn't had with anyone for years, that ranged from funny to serious, the basics of getting to know another person to the deeply intimate. Those conversations revealed that they'd both been seeking connection in their lives. And it'd all given Alex hope that, in the end, he'd been right to take this chance and let this man *in*.

And now, these gifts and these words turned that hope into resolve. Damn, he hated that Jamie had to leave, or he'd change his cuff tomorrow. But no matter, he could make it a surprise at the big New Year's Eve party next Sunday. That was the perfect time to take things to the next level.

When Alex broke the kiss, Jamie's eyes were soft and so fucking pretty. "Thank you, Sir. That…that means a lot."

A warm pressure filled Alex's chest. "Mmm, I want to wash you. Would you like that?"

"Uh, yeah. I mean, yes. Yes, Sir."

Alex chuckled and led him to one of the big shower stalls. And then he stripped his submissive down and took the most careful, tender care of him. Cleaning his body, washing his hair, massaging his shoulders and back. They didn't much speak, and Alex never made it sexual—though Jamie's very presence turned him on. But it still felt intimate beyond anything Alex had experienced with anyone else in a long, long time.

When they were done, Alex lent Jamie a pair of sweatpants. And then he stood before him and held out his wrist. "Would you hook the bracelet for me?"

"Yeah?" Jamie whispered.

He nodded and nailed him with a stare as he worked at the little clasp. Alex might be the sadist, but this man had the power to break him.

Or finally make him whole.

But as they said their good-byes and promised to text while they were apart, Alex refused to give into his old fears. Which just proved that Jamie Fielding was his weakness and his strength, too.

I can't wait to see you. What time do you land?

Phone in hand, Jamie lay sprawled on his parents' big sectional sofa in the family room, grinning like an idiot as he texted with Alex. His dad sat in his recliner watching a World War II documentary on The History Channel, and his mom was pulling together what smelled like a fantastic dinner.

He'd spent a great week with his family, celebrating Christmas, visiting old friends, and helping his parents out around the house, which was starting to become too much for his dad to handle on his own. Despite the good times and the beautiful weather and the home-cooked meals, Jamie was eager as fuck to head east tomorrow. Back to Baltimore. Back to Alex.

Too fucking late. Pushing 10, Jamie replied.

The little bubbles that indicated Alex was typing popped up immediately. *Come to my place when you get back. Stay with me tomorrow night.*

Jamie's stomach flipped. *Is that an order, Sir?*

The bubbles appeared and went away, appeared and went away, as if he was starting and stopping his words. Finally, *No. It's an invitation and a wish.* And then on the next line: *Don't want to wait to see you.*

There was that idiot grin again. Because he felt the same damn way. *Me either. And I'd love to stay with you.*

They'd been texting all week, and even sneaked in one

late-night call that'd turned into a scene where Master Alex had made Jamie edge himself—masturbate right up until the point of orgasm and then stop to make it back off again. In the end, he hadn't let Jamie come—the sadistic, sexy bastard—because he wanted Jamie wound tight when he returned.

Which seriously was *not* going to be a problem.

Especially since Alex had asked him to do a flogging demonstration with him at the big New Year's Eve party. On top of the anticipation of seeing Alex again was the nervous excitement of doing a scene in public again—this time as a demonstration.

So, yeah, Jamie would be wound *good* and tight.

His mom popped into the room. "The lasagna's browning, so just a few more minutes, boys."

Jamie peered toward the doorway. *Small but mighty* had always described his mom to a T. A social worker who'd fought for disadvantaged kids her whole life, she had gray hair that now matched the gray eyes that Jamie had inherited. "Thanks, Mom. Smells amazing. Need help?"

She planted her hands on her hips. "I'm not going to turn down a chance to hang out with you on your last night home. So sure."

Before pocketing his phone, he shot off one last text: *Almost dinner here. See you tomorrow night*

"Then put me to work," he said, hauling his lazy ass off the couch.

In the kitchen, she had him set the table and cut fresh, crusty bread into thick slices, and they worked for long minutes in amiable silence.

And then his mother asked, "What happened with you and Liz?"

Gathering up the plates and silverware, Jamie shrugged. "Just didn't work out."

Earlier in the week, he'd mentioned casually that they'd stopped seeing each other. But he hadn't had *any* idea what to say about Alex. If anything at all. Once he questioned whether he should tell them, however, he couldn't stop sitting and spinning on it. And, of course, it wasn't just his usual concerns of not wanting to build up their hopes and expectations around a relationship that was still new. It was also that he'd knock his parents sideways when he told them that he was with a *man*.

He had no idea how they'd react. Actually, he expected his mother to be cool. His dad, though? Jamie had no clue. His dad was old school, a navy man, the kind of guy who would, at once, give absolutely anyone the shirt off his back and, at the same time, rail against the news when he thought something was too politically correct.

And his parents had no reason to expect that Jamie might not be with a woman. Not when he was less than a week shy of his thirtieth birthday.

"Did you have a fight, or..." She shrugged. "I'm not trying to pry. I just want you to be happy. I can't see what's going on in your life when you're all the way across the country."

He arranged the last place-setting on the table. "I know. She and I had fun together, but we weren't as compatible as it first seemed."

"Well you'll find someone even better," Mom said, giving him a smile. Then she opened the oven door, revealing a bubbling pan of golden-grown cheese.

Jamie rushed over, eager to have something to do with his hands while his brain debated the wisdom of yelling out, *I already have!*

"Billy, dinner's ready," she called.

"Smells damn good in here, hon," Dad said when he joined them. He was a tall, thin man with an easy smile and ready laugh, at least most of the time.

Dinner conversation turned to light, easy topics. Jamie's job. Winter in Baltimore. His parents' planned trip to Hawaii in the spring. But the whole time, he was thinking about Alex.

If he couldn't share Alex with these two people, what did he think he was going to do in the rest of his life? His real life, outside the club and away from the community of people who were open to anything as long as it was safe, sane, and consensual.

Man up, Jamie.

It was the least Alex deserved from him. And the least he owed to deserve the man in return.

He set down his fork. Wiped his mouth. And spoke, "I want to share something with you guys. I've been wanting to all week, actually. But I'm leaving tomorrow and I don't want to go without you knowing."

"Everything okay, son?" his father asked, his brow furrowed.

Jamie smiled. "Actually, yeah. More than okay. I met someone a few weeks ago. It's still new, but it feels like it could be something."

His mother's smile was immediate. "Well, Jamie, that's great. Why didn't you say something when I was asking about Liz?"

He swallowed hard. "Because his name is Alex. Alex McGarry. He's a psychiatrist in Baltimore."

Mom's voice caught in her throat. Dad looked back and forth between Jamie and his wife, like he'd missed something. Jamie's gut clenched around the big square of lasagna he'd eaten.

"A man," Dad said.

He met his dad's confused gaze. "Yes, I'm dating a man. I really like him. I'm happier than I've been in a while."

"Okay, um," Mom began. "I'm just, I'm afraid you've caught us off guard. I'm glad that you're happy, of course. But are you saying you're gay?"

"Bi, actually. Bisexual, I mean," seeing the blankness in his father's expression. "It's not something I knew my whole life like some people do, I guess. It's something I've figured out. Anyway, I wanted you to know about Alex."

"I don't understand what bisexual is," Dad said, frowning. "I thought a person was either straight or gay."

How much he'd learned about sexuality, his and in general, during his short time of being a part of Blasphemy's community. And at the top of the list was the realization that sexuality was a spectrum, not a determination between a few set choices. "I'm not an expert in all this, Dad. I just know that I'm attracted to women and men. I think I have been for a while. And there was a lot I didn't question about myself that, looking back now, I see in a new light."

"Jesus, James. Is this just a phase or, I don't know, a midlife crisis at thirty?"

Jamie thought about Alex, and the question made him angry. "Not at all. In fact, I feel more serious about Alex than I've ever felt about anyone."

His dad chuffed out a laugh. "Well. Come on, son. That's not saying much given your track record."

"*Billy*," Mom chided. "That's enough."

"That's great, Dad. Thanks for the support." Jamie's throat went tight. He'd worried about his father's reaction, and it appeared he'd had good cause.

Mom raised her voice. It wasn't the first time she'd had to play referee between them. "Jamie. *Guys*. Just wait a minute. Of course we support you. And if Alex is important to you, that's all that matters to us. Right, Bill?"

The hesitation was a punch to the gut. "Sure," his father finally said. "So what are we supposed to tell people?"

His mother frowned. "Bill—"

But Jamie talked right over her because *are you fucking kidding me?* "Way to make this about you, Dad. Damnit, this is why I waited all week to say something."

"I'm just asking," Dad said, frustration clear in his tone. "I'm just trying to understand."

It didn't feel like that's what this was at all. "Why do you need to tell people anything? Just tell them your son's dating someone and seems happy. Or if you're feeling really adventurous, mention that your son has a boyfriend whom he really cares about."

"A *boyfriend*," he said, chuckling.

"Oh, for fuck's sake." Jamie threw up his hands and shoved out of his seat.

"Watch your mouth," Dad said.

Right. Because it was more important not to curse than it was to just accept your son for who and what he was—without belittling or criticizing or mocking.

Jamie turned on the tap to the sink. Rinsed the dirties that were within reach and loaded them into the dishwasher. His parents sat at the table whispering furiously. A quick peek showed that both of them were red-faced and angry. Great, so he'd caused a rift between them, too.

Finally, Dad left the table and the room without saying another word, and Mom came up and hugged Jamie from behind.

"I love you," she said. "And I'm happy for you."

"Thanks," Jamie said, smacking off the water. He turned and sagged against the counter, exhausted by the way that'd gone down.

"Your father's a stubborn old goat," Mom said. "He's behind you, too. Even though he fucked that up."

The comment both made Jamie chuff out a little laugh and brought stinging tears to the backs of his eyes. "He did," Jamie said.

It was a fuck-up that his father didn't rectify before Jamie departed early the next afternoon. Which made him even more glad that Alex had invited him to come directly to his house. Because in a few hours' time, he'd be right back where he belonged.

Chapter 11

A WEEK WAS A LONG TIME to be apart from someone when you'd just accepted that you were in love with them. Which was why Alex had been pacing and peeking out his front windows and checking his phone every five minutes since Jamie texted that he was leaving the airport.

It wasn't just that absence had made the heart grow fonder. And it hadn't really taken Jamie's departure to bring the emotions home. It was just that, in his solitude, Alex couldn't hide from the reality—and the intensity—of what was going on inside him.

That, somehow, he'd fallen in love with a man he'd only known for a few weeks. A man new to the lifestyle Alex had built his whole life around. A man new to having relationships with other men. A man ten years his junior who, having just found out so much about his sexuality, might not be ready to settle down. When that was *all* Alex wanted.

To settle down. With Jamie.

"Fuck," Alex bit out, peeking out the front window again. Because it was scary as hell to finally admit what he wanted. And to go after it.

Just then, a car pulled to the curb in front of Alex's little bungalow.

Jamie.

Alex flew out the front door. Off the porch. Down the sidewalk. And then he pinned the man he loved against the side of his Range Rover, raked his fingers into his short hair, and kissed him with every bit of emotion he felt. Jamie sank into the kiss, moaning and wrapping his arms around Alex's shoulders.

"That was the perfect way to come home," Jamie said when they broke apart.

"I'm glad you're here. Come on in." He took Jamie's carry-on roller bag and led him inside. "Hungry? Thirsty?"

Shaking his head, Jamie peered around, taking in his living room and the dining room beyond. The decor was a mix of the Mission style that coordinated with the house with some mid-century modern elements which more closely aligned with Alex's taste. "No, Sir. I'm just beat."

It was nearly eleven, so Alex couldn't blame him for that. But there was something he needed him to know. He stepped in close. "Unless we agree to do a scene, I'm just Alex here. You don't have to call me *Sir*. You don't have to kneel. You can speak freely. We're just two guys here."

Smiling, Jamie grasped his hips. "Okay, Alex."

Alex smiled, too. "I invited you over because I want to spend time with you before the party tomorrow night. Some time together outside of the club, you know?"

"I'd love that," Jamie said.

"Then how about we go to bed—" Jamie grinned. Alex laughed. "To *sleep*. And then we grab some brunch in the morning and maybe see a movie or something.

"And the sex? Where does that fit in?"

Chuckling, Alex shook his head. "I have some big things planned for you tomorrow night. I want you in *rare form*."

Jamie arched a brow. "I already *am* in rare form judging by the hard-on I have—from just being in your presence."

"You are temptation personified, do you know that?" Alex kissed Jamie again. "Let me lock up and then we can head upstairs." Alex gave the guy a tour of the place as he hit the lights, and man how he loved having Jamie here. He loved the company and the camaraderie and the energy.

Upstairs, they took turns in the bathroom, and then Alex turned down the covers on his big king-sized bed. "Do you have a favorite side?"

"I usually sleep on the right side, but since I'm probably just going to lay against you most of the night, it doesn't matter."

Alex did a double take at the image Jamie made standing in his bedroom doorway, naked except for a pair of form-fitting dark-blue cotton boxers. "I like the sound of that," he said. More than that, it was part of why he wanted to spend time with Jamie outside of the club. He felt so much affection for the guy, but sometimes he worried that, as a sadist, he didn't show enough of it. Tonight, it was all he wanted to do.

Stripping down to his own boxers, Alex gestured to the bed and watched as Jamie climbed in and made himself comfortable sitting up against the pillows. "What?" he asked.

"Just enjoying seeing you in my bed." Alex got in, too, and then held out an arm to invite Jamie to come closer.

He did. He fit his big body in along the nook of Alex's, his head coming to rest on his shoulder, one thigh pulled up atop Alex's legs. Alex wrapped an arm around Jamie's shoulders and pulled him even closer. They both sighed.

"How was the trip home? Family good?" Alex asked.

Jamie yawned and shifted closer still, close enough to feel that the man had a hard-on. "Yeah. I don't see them as much anymore since they live so far away. So it was good to get out there. Missed you though."

Alex pressed a kiss to Jamie's forehead. "So did I. I'm glad you're back."

"Me, too," Jamie said, his voice slurring from sleepiness. "I belong here…"

Alex's sentiments exactly, which he was about to say until the soft rumble of Jamie's breathing revealed that he'd fallen asleep. But he didn't mind. He didn't mind at all. Because he had the man he loved in his bed, in his arms, and in his home.

It was more than he'd thought he'd find. With anyone.

As the morning spilled gray light into the bedroom, Jamie realized two things. That he was still laying in the same position in which he'd fallen asleep—they both were. And that Alex's cock was erect against Jamie's thigh.

Which had Jamie immediately hard, his own cock tight against Alex's hip.

He peered up at the man and found him still asleep. He was torn between waking him up in some sexy way and respecting Alex's wishes that they couldn't have sex. But did that mean they couldn't do *anything*?

Jamie determined to test out the idea that they were just regular guys outside the club. Because a regular guy like, say, *him* would be all over that cock.

Moving slowly, he eased his boxers down his thighs

until he could push them off with his feet. He shifted positions to bring his body over Alex's and then he settled his weight on the other man so that their cocks were aligned. Grinding their cocks together nearly made Jamie moan.

"Aw, fuck," Alex said in a sleep-roughened voice. "That feels so good. You grinding on me is a stellar way to wake up."

Jamie smiled. "Couldn't help it. We were both hard and I couldn't keep my hands off you."

"Is that right?" Alex asked.

Nailing the other man with a stare, Jamie reached between them and pushed Alex's boxers down, too. Now their cocks rubbed skin to skin. "I missed feeling you. This big cock."

"Yeah," Alex rasped. He pulled Jamie down for a kiss. Soft and sweet at first, it quickly turned hot and aggressive. Their tongues plundered, their teeth nipped, their hands grasped tightly. And Jamie thrust their cocks together again and again.

"You look good underneath me, Alex," he said.

"Fuck, Jamie, get both of us off. Just like this."

On a groan, Jamie grasped onto Alex's shoulders, giving himself leverage to hump and grind and ride the man beneath him, the man he loved.

"Want my bed to smell like you," Alex said, his hands first grabbing at Jamie's shoulders, then his back, then his ass. "Like us."

Damn it all to hell, but Jamie wasn't going to last long. Not with the way Alex felt and the things he was saying. Jamie hunched his whole body around Alex so that they connected from knees to noses.

One stray errant thought did Jamie in—imagining that he was *penetrating* Alex instead of just dry humping him.

Jamie's orgasm hit him like a ton of bricks. "Gonna come, gonna come."

"Oh, yeah, babe. Oh yeah." The man's voice was strained and desperate.

His whole body contracting with the orgasm, Jamie moaned as his cock emptied a tremendous load over Alex's cock and belly.

"That's it," Alex bit out, his head writhing against the pillow. "I'm right behind you."

Jamie thrust harder, faster. Alex groaned. And then he was coming and cursing, their semen a sexy pool on Alex's flat belly.

"Jesus," Alex said, releasing a harsh breath. "Good morning."

Still laying atop him, Jamie grinned. "Good morning. And Happy New Year's Eve."

"Mmm, it's looking to be a good one, too. Every day should start this way." Alex waggled his brows.

Jamie nodded. "That might be able to be arranged." In fact, Jamie would be only too happy to share this man's bed.

Alex leaned up and kissed Jamie, thoroughly and lingeringly. "What do you say about some breakfast? There's a great diner with the best steak and eggs just a few blocks away."

"I'm fucking starved, so count me in." He really hadn't eaten dinner the night before, not unless the flight's peanuts and shortbread cookies counted.

They made quick work of cleaning up and getting dressed, and then they walked the short distance from Alex's house to the diner, one of those fifties-looking places with bright red booths and stools, a juke box at every table, and a massive dessert case that filled the front of the store.

They both got the steak and eggs. And then they talked and ate and laughed and joked like they'd known each other for *years*. It almost felt that way to Jamie, except he'd never be able to forget what a special, rare thing it'd been for him to find someone with whom he connected on so many levels.

The only thing Jamie wanted to share with Alex but hadn't yet was how his conversation with his parents had gone. It'd eaten at him the whole flight home. And only sheer exhaustion had prevented him from telling Alex last night—well, that and a desire not to walk in and immediately dump a problem on the guy. He'd been way too excited about going to Alex's for the first time—and his first time spending the night—to want to start things off that way.

But he did want to tell Alex and resolved to do it when they returned to the privacy of his house.

When the bill came, Alex grabbed it. "You're my guest, this is my treat."

"Okay," Jamie said. "Then next time's on me. How about next Tuesday night for dinner? Any chance you're free?"

"I need to check my schedule at Blasphemy, but I'm sure I can make something work. What's Tuesday?"

Jamie ducked his chin. "My thirtieth birthday."

Alex grinned. "You're not treating on your own fucking birthday."

"Yes, I am. That was the deal. Besides, if I have you, there won't be a single other thing I need."

"Have I told you lately how dangerous your mouth is?" Alex said, a hint of sternness to his tone that heated Jamie's blood.

Jamie chuckled. "Well I guess the question, *Alex*, is what you're going to do about that little problem."

They rose from the booth, laughing as Alex threatened to meet that challenge *tonight.* Alex paid at the old-time register, and then they spilled out onto the street and Alex took Jamie by the hand.

They turned the corner to go back to Alex's and nearly walked headlong into two people coming the opposite direction.

Oh shit. Not just any two people either. One of the senior partners of Jamie's law firm and his wife.

"A boyfriend!" The memory of his own father's mocking tone flashed through his head.

Jamie pulled his hand free from Alex's.

Time slowed to a crawl. The decision to pull away. The flash of hurt in Alex's dark eyes. Larry Katz exclaiming his surprise at running into Jamie here—literally.

"Uh, yes, sir. Quite a surprise. My friend lives in the neighborhood, and he sold me with his description of the steak and eggs. Alex, Larry's one of the senior partners at my firm."

Alex gave a polite smile. "I'm the *friend*."

Larry chuckled and extended his hand. Introduced himself. Alex did the same.

And all the while Jamie could barely breathe for the boulder of embarrassment and regret that parked itself on his chest. Not embarrassment about being with Alex. Embarrassment and shame in himself for letting what his father said—or hadn't said—get to him. Worse, for allowing the insecurity that whole episode had unleashed inside him to hurt the man he loved.

Because he could see it on Alex's face. Not anger. *Disconnection.*

Like the shutters had gone down over his eyes.

The moment they were alone again, Jamie turned to Alex. "I'm sorry. I handled that all wrong."

"Yes, you did." Hands in his coat pockets, Alex started walking.

Jamie hustled to catch up. "Alex, wait. Let me explain."

Shaking his head, Alex chuffed out a humorless laugh. "That was all completely self-explanatory."

Icy foreboding crawled down Jamie's spine. There had to be something he could say to make this better.

By the time they were back to Alex's, the man still hadn't said a single word. He whirled on him when they made it to his living room.

"I'm almost forty years old, Jamie. I have known who and what I am for most of those forty years. And under no circumstances can I ever accept anyone who's ashamed of me or can't accept me."

"I accept you completely," Jamie said, the words opening up a jagged hole near his heart.

"Really? Is that what you just did? The very first time we're out in public together, the very first time we run into someone you know, and you couldn't get your hand out of mine fast enough."

"Alex, I messed up. I know I did. I knew it the second I did it. I just kinda panicked." Alarmed goosebumps raced over his skin, because this was not going well. And Alex wasn't just angry, he was *hurt*.

Alex released a long breath and shook his head. The look in his eyes was so distant that Jamie hurt, too. "I get it. You're new at all this. You're probably not ready for everyone in your life to know. That makes sense for you. But it doesn't make sense for me, Jamie."

"Jesus, Alex. Wait—"

"So please collect your belongings and go. And I don't want to see you at Blasphemy tonight."

If Alex had hit him it would've hurt less. "You don't… want me?"

Alex shook his head. "No, but I wish you well."

Chapter 12

JAMIE WASN'T TAKING *NO* FOR an answer. Honestly, he didn't really have a choice. Because Alex breaking up with him had left him shattered. Half way home, he'd had to pull over on the side of the road and throw up his breakfast. After that, he couldn't eat anything. Couldn't drink, even water, without getting nauseous. Couldn't sleep. Couldn't sit still.

He just kept seeing Alex's dead eyes and his flat tone and his utter fucking disappointment and hurt replay on the inside of his mind again and again.

Jamie had to make this better.

So he went to Blasphemy. At the black double doors outside the church, he smiled at the security guard he now knew by name. "Hey, Carlos. Happy New Year's Eve," Jamie said.

Carlos smiled, but then his expression changed. "Hey, Jamie. Your name's not on the list."

"Can you double check? My provisional membership is supposed to be good through tomorrow."

Carlos clicked through some screens on a tablet. "I'm sorry, Jamie. Your membership was terminated early."

Jamie couldn't breathe. The finality of that was devastating. He just blinked and stumbled away in a near-stupor. Alex hadn't just disinvited him from the party, he'd cancelled his membership. He'd cut him out of his life and out of his club.

I don't want to see you at Blasphemy…

Jamie stared up at the club for long minutes. Maybe an hour. He had no idea what to do with himself or where to go. Somehow he made it home, inside, to his bed.

Monday morning came, but it was New Year's Day so he had off work. Which was good because he never got out of bed all day. Until that night, when he had an idea he couldn't resist.

This is the waiting position, which is also good when you've made a mistake and wish to display contrition.

Jamie had make a mistake. And he wanted to display contrition with every fiber of his being.

He drove to Blasphemy, went to about the very spot he'd stood in that first night when he'd admired the hidden church behind the public dance club, and got on his knees.

Knees spread, palms up, head down.

And then he waited, because *that* was the only thing he could do. The only thing that felt right. The only thing that felt like anything at all.

He had no idea how long he'd been kneeling there when someone approached. Two women. "Are you okay?"

"Yes, Ma'am," he said, shivering. "I'm waiting."

They left him, and a short while later, a man approached. He crouched down. Carlos. "Jamie, I'm going to have to ask you to leave."

He shook his head. "I'm waiting."

"I can't let you stay here, man. It's private property. I

don't want to call the police on you, and I don't think you want that either."

"Please let me stay."

"I can't. You have to go," Carlos said, sympathy in his tone.

His chest felt so hollow he could barely breathe. He forced himself up, but his legs were utterly numb and he stumbled and went down hard. Carlos sat with him until he could try again. And then Jamie drove around the city until his car somehow made it back to his home.

On Tuesday, he called out of work so he didn't have to get out of bed. And on Tuesday night, he went back to Blasphemy. And he knelt because he'd made a mistake and wanted to show contrition.

This time, he made it about two hours, and then Carlos was back, but he wasn't alone. Master Kyler hauled him off the ground and sat him on a bench to force the circulation back into his legs.

"I don't know what happened, Jamie, and I respect the hell out of what you're trying to do here. But you can't keep coming back. Your membership is over, and this is a private club."

"There's nothing else I can do, Master Kyler. I made a mistake. Now I have to show contrition."

Kyler sighed. "I can't believe I'm asking this, because he's gonna *kill* me. But what kind of mistake?"

Shame set his face on fire, despite the cold January temperature that'd seeped into his bones. "I pulled my hand from his when I saw someone I knew. A partner at my firm. It was such a dick move."

Master Kyler groaned. "Shit, kid."

"Yeah. The thing is, though, that I came out to my parents two days before. And my dad..." Jamie shook his head. "His reaction wasn't what I hoped. So it doesn't make what I did any better, but my head was screwed up."

"Does Master Alex know this?" the Dom asked.

"I never got a chance to tell him."

Master Kyler rose. "Okay, Jamie. Go home. That's an order. It's too fucking cold for you to be sitting out here."

Jamie did as he was told. Drove around again for hours rather than be alone with him shame and his pain.

The next morning, he woke up in his bed not remembering how he'd gotten there. Jesus, what if Alex refused to ever even speak to him again? Would Jamie always feel this way?

He sent his head of HR another message that he wasn't coming in. Which was when he noticed the date. January third. His birthday.

Just a few short days ago he'd been making plans with the man he loved for this night, and now he was all alone. Unable to think of what else to do, he went back to the courtyard outside of Blasphemy again. Found his spot. It had snowed a little overnight, so he took off his coat and spread it on the icy ground.

And then he knelt. And waited.

"He's back," Master Kyler said. "You need to handle this."

Alex glared at his friend, who'd been harping on him for two days. "I'm working, Master Kyler." He gestured to the membership registration desk. "As you can see."

"Fuck that, Alex. Go make this right."

Alex shot up from his seat. "This isn't your fucking business, Vance."

"No? Last I checked this club was one-twelfth mine.

You were my friend. And the kid who's been kneeling out in the snow for the past two hours joined on my recommendation." He held out his hands as his volume rose. "That all feels like my business."

The mention of the snow threatened to unleash a pang of sympathy, but Alex beat it back. He had no sympathy, not after all he'd risked. And all he'd lost. Just like he'd fucking known he would. "You don't even know what—"

"I know more than you think." Kyler arched a brow over those bright blue eyes.

Alex blanched. "What the hell does that mean?"

"Did you know Jamie came out to his parents and it didn't go well with his father?"

That news was like a one-two punch to the gut. One, that it'd happened. Two, that Kyler knew when Alex didn't. "How do you know that?"

"Because I talked to Jamie. Which is what you need to do." He nailed him with an icy-blue stare.

All of a sudden, Master Quinton came barreling into the registration area, punching his arms into a coat. "It's fucking sleeting out there now. I'm not letting him stay out there any longer. I've been keeping an eye on the security cams and he looks drenched." He pointed a finger at Alex. "You don't want to handle this tonight. Fine. I'll take care of him. But you fix this. It's fucking January third. It's too dangerous for him to be out there in weather like this. Make sure it's the last time."

January third.

January third? Why did that—

"Christ, it's his birthday," Alex rasped.

Quinton and Kyler froze. "What?" Kyler asked.

"Aw, are you fucking kidding me?" Quinton growled.

"It's his birthday," Alex said, his gut twisting and the

room spinning and his heart throbbing like it'd been doing every one of the past three days. Since Jamie's actions had confirmed Alex's biggest fears.

No. Maybe, just maybe, since Jamie's actions *seemed* to confirm Alex's biggest fears.

Because, Jesus, he'd come out to his parents. That was huge. And he'd had to deal with a less-than-supportive reaction. And yet…there was nothing before the moment when he'd pulled his hand away that'd even once indicated any embarrassment or shame in being out in public with him. Alex was certain of it, since he'd replayed the whole morning over and over in his head a million times.

"*Alex*," Quinton said.

But he was already moving. "I'll get him. Jesus Christ, I'll get him." He stopped short and reached out a hand. "Give me your coat."

Quinton shrugged out of it, and then Alex *ran*.

He raced through the frigid night and skidded to a stop in front of Jamie, literally, because everything was covered in ice. Including Jamie, who had a dripping wet wool coat over his head and shoulders.

"Fuck, Jamie. Are you trying to hurt yourself?" Alex said, his heart a wild, desperate thing in his chest. He pulled off the wet coat and helped Jamie put Quinton's dry one on with the hood up and the front secured.

"Master Alex," he rasped. "I made a mistake. And I wanted you to see my contrition. Just like you said."

The words—and the ache that infused them—were like a steel knife to Alex's windpipe. He drowned in them until he couldn't breathe. "Dear God, you're so cold. Put your arm around my shoulders. We're going in."

"I'm sorry," Jamie said as he swayed and sagged. "So sorry."

"Sshh, baby. It's all right. Everything's all right." Alex lifted the man into his arms, willing it to be so. "Hold on to my neck, Jamie. Just hold on."

Kyler and Quinton exploded out of the doors to help. "I cleared out the locker room and started one of the showers for you," Kyler said. "Should be nice and hot."

"And I have a pot of coffee coming," Quinton said. "But if we need to get an ambulance over here, let me know."

Kyler held one set of doors, and Quinton the other. And then Kyler held open the door to the locker room and nailed him with a stare. "Take care of him."

Alex's throat went tight. No one would ever have to tell him that again.

But all that mattered right this second was getting Jamie warm. Clouds of steam filled the air, and Alex made for the running shower. He stepped in, not caring at all that both of them were fully clothed.

He came out to his parents.

"Can you stand yet, Jamie? I need to take off these frozen clothes so we can warm you up."

With some effort, he did, though he continued to use Alex's body to keep himself steady. Alex didn't mind that one bit. Especially as a sneaking tendril of guilt started snaking through him. One that said if Jamie got hurt or sick from this, it was Alex's fault.

Slowly but surely, he undressed Jamie, until the hot water could finally reach his skin and begin to warm him. Jamie shivered and groaned. But it was better than the silence of moments before.

Finally, Jamie's skin warmed, his lips pinked up, and he could stand on his own. And he looked everywhere but at Alex.

"Look at me, Jamie. Please."

He did, and his eyes went glassy and his face crumpled. "I'm so sorry," he rasped. "I didn't mean to hurt you, but I know I did. But I could never, ever be ashamed of you."

God, Alex had done this, had snuffed out this kid's light. And he hated himself for it.

"I know what happened with your parents, Jamie. I'm really sorry to hear that your dad didn't take it well. But I understand now why you panicked when you saw your senior partner. And if I'd only given you time to explain…" Alex shook his head, so disappointed in himself. Because he'd let fear get the best of him. And he'd hurt the person he loved as a result of it.

"It's not an excuse, I know," Jamie said, gaze lowered. "But I'm glad you know about it. Because I couldn't live with myself if you thought I was ashamed of you."

"You tried to tell me. I didn't listen. That's on me." And, *fuck*, it really was.

He was the one who made the mistake.

Alex should be the one down on his knees, which was exactly what he did. "*I'm* the one who needs to apologize for making a mistake."

Jamie's eyes went wide and his jaw dropped open.

"Can you forgive me, Jamie?" Suddenly, his heart was a thundering bass beat in his chest.

"Always," Jamie said, his voice so full of anguish.

Alex crawled forward until he knelt so close that he had to tilt back his head to make eye contact. Emotion sat thick in his throat. "Please forgive me."

"Of course, I do," Jamie whispered. "How could I not? I love you."

Everything inside Alex froze, righted itself, began to heal. "Fuck, Jamie. After everything, you love me?"

"I do."

"Jesus, baby, I love you, too." And damn if it felt good

to finally admit that. He was long overdue.

"What?" Jamie collapsed back against the tile behind him. "W-what did you say?"

Alex pulled Jamie down until they knelt face to face. "That I love you. And I was so scared that you might not love me back that I pushed you away at the slightest sign of trouble. God, I'm so fucking sorry."

"So, what does this mean?" Jamie asked quietly, the rain of the shower nearly drowning him out.

"I'd like it to mean a second chance. What do you want it to mean?" Alex asked, his heart in Jamie's hands. Where he hoped it might always be.

Those gray eyes appraised him. "A second chance for...?"

"For everything," Alex said.

"Everything," Jamie whispered. "Together."

"Yes," Alex said. "I want you as my partner, as my submissive, and as my friend. And I wouldn't complain if you were my roommate either because I loved waking up with you in my arms. I'm looking for forever, Jamie."

"I want to be that for you," Jamie said, swallowing thickly.

"Oh, baby, don't you understand yet? You already are." Alex kissed him then, a sweet, slow, soul-healing kiss. It went on and on until they were breathless and the water went from hot to warm.

"Let's get you dried off and into some warm clothes. And Quinton brought coffee," Alex said, needing to take care of Jamie the same way he needed his next breath.

A few minutes later, they were dry and warm, dressed in borrowed clothing Kyler had left, and sitting together on a bench in the locker room with cups of coffee in hand.

Jamie was quiet for a long moment, and then he chuffed

out a little laugh. "We fucked that up big time."

Alex laughed. He actually laughed. Which just a few short hours before would've been an utter impossibility. "Yeah, we really fucking did."

Shifting closer on the bench, Jamie finally met his gaze with eyes free of the agony that'd cast shadows there not long before. "But if we're going for forever, there's going to be fucking up."

Nodding, Alex took Jamie's free hand. Because he couldn't stop touching him, each caress proof that Jamie was here and okay. "Yeah, I guess that's true."

"Which means that what's really important is fighting through the fuck ups and coming out the other side."

So damn brave, this kid. "Yes. And I promise you I will always fight for you, Jamie. I'll never leave you to fight on your own again."

"Then can we go home, Alex? Because I was so scared I'd lost you. And now that I know I didn't, I just want to be with the man I love and have him hold me in his arms," Jamie said.

Alex was so overwhelmed by the way this night was turning out. Overwhelmed by Jamie and this love they'd found. He pulled Jamie up, and they made for the door. "Yes, baby, let's go home. Because forever starts right now. And I'm never wasting another moment of it again."

Epilogue

Love is Love is Love
James Edward Fielding
and
Alexander Michael McGarry
Invite you to share in the joy of their wedding day
Saturday, the eleventh of August
Two Thousand Eighteen
At five o'clock in the evening
Dinner and Dancing to Follow

She's Here!
Catherina Noelle Fielding-McGarry
Born May 1, 2019 in Rio de Janeiro, Brazil
Finally home on July 7, 2022
Overjoyed, Jamie & Alex

Acknowledgements

I HOPE YOU ENJOYED THIS NEWEST story in the Blasphemy series! And I hope you'll join my VIP Readers – because I'd love to share all kinds of fun exclusives with you!

I adored writing Alex and Jamie's story, and loved the process of self-discovery they both went through. Sometimes we all need to find that person who can help us understand who and what we are, or how to get to where we need to be. And I found that powerfully relatable as I was writing these characters.

I have a number of people who I absolutely must thank! First, my very good author friends, Christi Barth and Lea Nolan, who selflessly threw themselves into commenting and proofreading and helping me make *On His Knees* shine. I love these ladies like sisters and appreciate all they do for me so much.

I must also thank KP Simmon, who is an amazing giver of pep talks.

Certainly, this book would not have been finished without the patience of my husband and kids, who encouraged me to go work and cheered me on when I finished. My family is an amazing source of support, and I couldn't do what I love without them.

Or without all of you. Thanks, as always, to my Heroes

and my Reader Girls. And thank YOU, dear reader, for taking my characters into your heart and allowing them to tell their stories over and over again. ~LK

Coming Soon from Laura Kaye...

THE WARRIOR FIGHT CLUB SERIES

Starting with
FIGHTING FOR EVERYTHING

A new contemporary series of standalone romances about an MMA training club that helps veterans deal with PTSD and transition to civilian life.

The first in this new series is coming May 22, 2018!

ABOUT FIGHTING FOR EVERYTHING

Loving her is the biggest fight of his life…

Home from the Marines, Noah Cortez has a secret he doesn't want his oldest friend, Kristina Moore, to know. It kills him to push her away, especially when he's noticing just how sexy and confident she's become in his absence. But, angry and full of fight, he's not the same man anymore either. Which is why Warrior Fight Club sounds so good.

Kristina loves teaching, but she wants more out of life. She wants Noah—the boy she's crushed on and waited for. Except Noah is all man now—in ways both oh so good and troubling, too. Still, she wants who he's become—every war-hardened inch. And when they finally stop fighting their attraction, it's everything Kristina never dared hope for.

But Noah is secretly spiraling, and when he lashes out, it threatens what he and Kristina have found. The brotherhood of the fight club helps him confront his demons, but only Noah can convince the woman he loves that he's finally ready to fight for everything.

PREORDER NOW!

About the Blasphemy Series

AN EROTIC ROMANCE SERIES OF STANDALONES…

From the ruins of a church comes Baltimore's most exclusive club

12 Masters. Infinite Fantasies.
Welcome to Blasphemy…

BOOKS IN SERIES:
HARD TO SERVE
BOUND TO SUBMIT
MASTERING HER SENSES
EYES ON YOU
THEIRS TO TAKE
ON HIS KNEES

HARD TO SERVE (HARD INK #5.5/BLASPHEMY #.5)
To protect and serve is all Detective Kyler Vance ever wanted to do, so when Internal Affairs investigates him as part of the new police commissioner's bid to oust corruption, everything is on the line. Which makes meeting smart, gorgeous submissive, Mia Breslin, at an exclusive

play club the perfect distraction. Their scorching scenes lure them to play together again and again. But then Kyler runs into Mia at work and learns that he's been dominating the daughter of the hard-ass boss who has it in for him. Now Kyler must choose between life-long duty and forbidden desire before Mia finds another who's not so hard to serve.

Bound to Submit (Blasphemy #1)
FREE ON ALL RETAILERS

He thinks he caused her pain, but she knows he's the only one who can heal her…

Kenna Sloane lost her career and her arm in the Marines, and now she feels like she's losing herself. Submission is the only thing that ever freed her from pain and made her feel secure, and Kenna needs to serve again. Bad. The only problem is the Dom she wants once refused her submission and broke her heart, but, scarred on the inside and out, she's not looking for love this time. She's not even sure she's capable. Griffin Hudson is haunted by the mistakes that cost him the only woman he ever loved. Now she's back at his BDSM club, Blasphemy, and more beautiful than ever, and she's asking for his help with the pain he knows he caused. Even though he's scared to hurt her again, he can't refuse her, because he'd give anything to earn a second chance. And this time, he'll hold on forever.

Mastering Her Senses (Blasphemy #2)

He wants to dominate her senses—and her heart…

Quinton Ross has always been a thrill-seeker—so it's no surprise that he's drawn to extremes in the bedroom and at his BDSM club, Blasphemy, where he creates sense-depriving scenarios that blow submissives' minds.

Now if he could just find one who needs the rush as much as him... Cassia Locke hasn't played at Blasphemy since a caving accident left her with a paralyzing fear of the dark. Ready to fight, she knows just who to ask for help—the hard-bodied, funny-as-hell Dom she'd always crushed on—and once stood up. Quinton is shocked and a little leery to see Cassia, but he can't pass up the chance to dominate the alluring little sub this time. Introducing her to sensory deprivation becomes his new favorite obsession, and watching her fight fear is its own thrill. But when doubt threatens to send her running again, Quinton must find a way to master her senses—and her heart.

EYES ON YOU (BLASPHEMY #3)

She wants to explore her true desires, and he wants to watch...

When a sexy stranger asks Wolf Henrikson to rescue her from a bad date, he never expected to want the woman for himself. But their playful conversation turns into a scorching one-night stand that reveals the shy beauty gets off on the idea of being seen, even if she's a little scared of it, too. And Wolf loves to watch. In the wake of discovering her fiancé's infidelity, florist Olivia Foster never expected to find someone who not only understood her wildest, darkest fantasies, but would bring them to life. As Wolf introduces her to his world at the play club, Blasphemy, Liv finds herself tempted to explore submission and exhibitionism with the hard-bodied Dom even as she's scared to trust again. But Wolf is a master of getting what he wants—and he's got his eyes set on her...

THEIRS TO TAKE (BLASPHEMY #4)

She's the fantasy they've always wanted to share...

Best friends Jonathan Allen and Cruz Ramos share

almost everything—a history in the Navy, their sailboat building and restoration business, and the desire to dominate a woman together, which they do at Baltimore's exclusive club, Blasphemy. Now if they could find someone who wants to play for keeps…All Hartley Farren has in the world is the charter sailing business she inherited from her beloved father. So when a storm damages her boat, she throws herself on the mercy of business acquaintances to do the repairs—stat. She never expected to find herself desiring the sexy, hard-bodied builders, but being around Jonathan and Cruz reminds Hartley of how much she longs for connection. If only she could decide which man she wants to pursue more…As their attraction flashes hot, Jonathan and Cruz determine to have Hartley for their own. But the men's erotic world is new and overwhelming, and Hartley's unsure if she could really submit to being both of theirs to take… forever.

ON HIS KNEES (BLASPHEMY #5)

Getting on his knees makes him question everything…and want even more…

Another failed relationship has lawyer Jamie Fielding confronting the truth—he'll never be satisfied with any woman until he admits what he needs…to submit and to be used—hard. When a friend invites him to the exclusive Blasphemy club, Jamie is stunned to find everything he ever wanted—in the fierce, ruthless hands of a man. Psychiatrist Alex McGarry will play with anyone who craves his rough brand of domination, but what he really wants is to settle down. Which makes the submissive male he meets at his club a bad idea—the man might be hot as hell but he's also new to everything Alex has to offer. Except that doesn't keep them from coming together again and again, sating every one of their darkest desires. Master Alex sets Jamie's whole world on fire and makes him question everything—and that's good. Because Alex won't tolerate hiding what they have for long and he wants much more than just having Jamie on his knees...

NEED MORE MASTERS?
Read on to meet Master Jonathan and Master Cruz in:

THEIRS TO TAKE

Chapter 1

HARTLEY FARREN STARED AT THE wreck of her catamaran and tried not to cry. Or scream. Or punch something with her bare fist.

She'd done everything right to prepare for the hurricane that had come through two days before. Baltimore's Lighthouse Point's marina provided an excellent safe harbor with a fantastic track record of low storm damage, and she'd been sure to use long dock lines to allow the boat to rise and fall during the storm surge. But none of that mattered when someone *else* wasn't as diligent in their preparations. And the consequence had been that another boat had lost its mooring and the wind had driven it into her *Far 'n Away*, damaging the port side.

"I'm really sorry," the other owner said for the dozenth time. "I told Charlie we needed more lines, but he said the Chesapeake never gets hit that badly." In her sixties and sweet as pie, the lady made it hard for Hartley to stay mad when she revealed that their own boat, a total loss, had been their only residence for the past eighteen months, leaving them essentially homeless. They stood and watched while the lady's husband worked with the harbor master to have the wreck towed away.

"I know," Hartley said. "It'll all work out somehow. For both of us."

Hartley had to believe that. Because that cat was her whole life.

Her father had left his charter business to her when he died three years before. Now, that business and that boat provided her whole income and allowed her to keep her grandmother, who suffered from Alzheimer's, in a lovely assisted-living community.

But now Hartley was dead in the water. Or, at least, her charter business was. Until she dealt with the insurance claims and found someone to do the repairs. Both were sure to be a pain in the butt following a big storm.

Hartley sighed. Neither crying, screaming, nor punching something was going to make anything better. And she'd certainly fared better than some others—she had to be grateful for that. She slid the business card detailing the couple's contact information into her pocket and said her good-byes, and then she made her way to the marina office.

"Hi Linda," she said to the office manager she'd met for the first time when she was only eight or nine. Back then, Hartley had been her dad's "first mate" as much as going to school and playing field hockey had allowed.

"How bad is it, hon?" Linda tucked the gray hair of her bob behind her ears as she came around her desk. The office was a big square with four desks, the back two partially hidden behind cubicle partitions. Normally, the room was bright and airy, as windows lined the two exterior walls, but boards currently covered the glass, making it feel like nighttime in the middle of the day.

"Fixable. That's not the problem, though. The problem is whether it can be fixed fast. There's no avoiding having to cancel several weeks of charters, but I'll be sunk if I have to pull out of the sailboat show and the Sailing University courses I'm teaching."Thank God she'd been smart enough to buy business interruption insurance, but that was only going to cover her so far. If she didn't get the *Far 'n Away* repaired within three weeks, well, she wasn't going to think about that. Not yet.

"What can I do to help?" Linda asked, giving her the same affectionate, grandmotherly look she'd been giving her for the past twenty-plus years. It was an affection born not only from their long-time friendship, but from the fact that Linda and her father had been close—close enough that Hartley suspected something romantic between them before her dad unexpectedly died of a heart attack. Since then, Linda had been one of the few people who seemed to understand the grief and loneliness Hartley had been working through.

"Can I borrow a desk and your Wi-Fi?" Hartley gestured to the messenger bag on her shoulder. "I have my laptop and I'd love to dive into finding a place that can do the work."

"That's easy. Of course. You know your way around. Make yourself at home."

"Thanks, Linda. What would I do without you?" she asked as she sat at the more private desk behind Linda's.

The older lady peered around the corner at her and smirked. "Says the woman who spends days and days alone at sea. You'd get by just fine. You don't *need* me, Hartley. I'm just your cheerleading section."

Hartley chuckled. "Well, I appreciate that, too." She set up and turned on her laptop. She'd just looked up the contact information for her insurance company when Linda placed a steaming mug on the desk.

"I'm also your deliverer of mint tea." Linda winked.

"And clearly also a goddess," Hartley said, taking the cup in hand. She adored the feeling of warm ceramic against her palms. "Can't forget that one."

"Naturally," Linda said. "Hey, since you're here, can you let anyone who comes in know I'll be right back? I have to run over to the Harbor Master's office for a short meeting."

"You got it," Hartley said, sipping at the sweet, minty tea. A moment later, the front door opened and closed, leaving Hartley alone to figure out who was going to be her savior.

Scheduling a time to meet with the insurance adjuster turned out to be easy enough. But, thirty minutes later, she'd called a dozen boat repair shops and only found two willing to consider the work—but neither could even come look at the cat for almost a week, nor commit to completing the repairs within the next three.

Hartley dropped her head into her hands and heaved a deep breath. In the quiet, the soft opening and closing of the outer door reached her ears. "Hey, Linda," she called. Then, to herself, "What am I going to do?"

"Hey, are you okay?"

The voice was deep, male, and definitely not Linda's. Hartley's gaze whipped up. And up. To find a tall and incredibly sexy man standing in the doorway to her cubicle. Sun-kissed shoulder-length blond hair framed a ruggedly masculine face and intense gray eyes that were at once inquisitive and observing. Broad shoulders and defined muscles pulled taut a heather-gray T-shirt with a single word across the chest: *NAVY*. His forearms and legs beneath khaki cargo shorts were toned and tanned, as if he spent a lot of time in the sun.

"Uh, hi. Yes. Sorry. I'm kinda in my own world here. Did you need Linda?" Hartley managed as she pushed to her feet. At five-five, she wasn't short, but his impressive height made her tilt her head back to meet his assessing gaze.

He shook his head. "I was coming by to see if she needed a hand with anything around the marina."

"Oh. Wow. I'm sure she'd appreciate that. She stepped out to a meeting but she should be back soon if you'd like to wait." Despite his selfless reason for being there, the man made Hartley nervous. She wasn't sure why. Maybe it was the intensity behind those odd, gray eyes. Or the way he towered over her. Or how freaking good-looking he was.

"I'll do that. Thanks."

"Sure," she said. But he didn't leave. "Um, anything else I can do for you?"

His gaze stayed glued to hers, but she had the oddest feeling that he was checking her out nonetheless. He smiled and shook his head. And, *man*, was his smile a stunner, highlighting the strong angles of his jaw and charming her with the way the right side of his mouth lifted higher than the left. He thumbed over his shoulder. "I'll just grab a seat."

And then he disappeared from her little doorway.

Hartley was half tempted to peer around the corner and watch him walk away. Just to see if the rear view was as impressive as the front.

On a sigh, she dropped back into her chair. And even though her thoughts should've returned to the huge problem of fixing her boat, they lingered on the Good Samaritan currently making small noises on the other side of the room. Who was he? Hartley had essentially grown up around this marina. Even though she couldn't say she knew everyone here, she still recognized most of the regulars. And she'd never seen Mr. Tall, Blond, and

Ruggedly Handsome before.

Her cell phone buzzed, pulling her from her thoughts.

"Hello?" she answered.

"Mrs. Farren, this is Ed Stark returning your call from Stark Restoration."

Hope rushed through Hartley. "Hi, Mr. Stark. Thanks for calling back so quickly. And, please, call me Hartley." Being called 'missus' was almost laughable when she couldn't remember the last time she'd gone on a date. With rebuilding the business after her father's death and taking care of her grandmother, Hartley didn't have time to date. Or, at least, she hadn't made the time. Not that she'd had any prospects motivating her to do so. Shaking the thoughts away, she filled the man in on the damage and the challenge of her timeline.

"I might be able to get someone out to take a look at your boat by the end of the week, but you're at least the tenth call I've had today. I wouldn't be able to guarantee a completion date without assessing the damage, and I've got a number of other repair jobs ahead of yours."

It was the same thing all the others had told her. And Hartley got it. She did. It wasn't anyone else's problem that she depended on the *Far 'n Away* for her livelihood. Or that she'd put most of what her father left her three years ago into her grandmother's nursing home and a bigger boat that could carry more passengers. Or that July had been so rainy that her normal charter business had been halved. Or that she needed the extra income that the sailboat show and Sailing University courses would bring in to make it through the leaner winter months.

Just then, the front door opened again. "Hartley, I'm back. Sorry I was gone so long." This time, it was definitely Linda. "Oh, Jonathan. How are you? How did you guys make out in the storm?"

"Our shop's fine, ma'am," the man said. "Thanks for asking." Jonathan. Jonathan who apparently had a shop somewhere in the marina?

Even more curious about him, Hartley stepped out of her cubicle and tried not to stare. Or drool. She forced her gaze to her friend. "Hey, Linda. Everything go okay?"

"Oh, yes. Just little fires everywhere that need put out," Linda said, dropping a legal pad full of notes onto her desk. "Were you able to find anyone to do the work?"

Hartley's shoulders fell. "No. No one can even look before Friday." And with a hole in the side of the cat, who knew how much more damage it might sustain over those four days.

Linda frowned, and then her gaze swung to Jonathan. "Have you two met yet?"

That intense gray-eyed gaze landed on Hartley, unleashing a whirl of butterflies in her belly. "Haven't had the pleasure to do so officially," Jonathan said.

It was a simple statement. But something about the word *pleasure* from that man's mouth made a tingle run down her spine. It'd clearly been too long since she'd been on a date. Or been kissed. And waaaay too long since she'd last had sex. Embarrassingly long. Like, she didn't even want to admit to herself how long.

(Fifteen months. Oy.)

With that fantastic thought in mind, all Hartley managed to say was, "Uh, hi. Again." *Wow, that was some brilliant conversation right there, Hartley.* She chuckled to cover how much she wanted to duck back into the cubicle and bang her head against the desk.

He grinned. "Hi. Again. I'm Jonathan Allen."

"Hartley Farren." Feeling Linda's amused gaze on her, she cleared her throat. "You have a shop in the marine center?"

He nodded. "A&R Builds and Restoration."

"Jonathan and his partner Cruz own the business that moved into the old Stanton space at the beginning of the summer," Linda added helpfully.

Hartley's eyes went wide as her heart kicked into a sprint. "*You* do builds and restoration?"

He chuckled. "As the name suggests."

She didn't mind the teasing, not when he might be able to help her. "Then you might be my new favorite person."

"Is that right?"

The office phone rang, and Linda excused herself to answer it.

Hartley stepped closer to Jonathan. Why did that make her feel like she was approaching a usually friendly but sometimes lethal animal? Her stomach did a little flip. "Yes, because I need a huge, huge, *gigantic* favor."

He arched a sexy brow. "And if I do this favor, will I *officially* be your favorite person?"

She grinned, enjoying his playfulness—and the fact that he was entertaining doing her a favor when they barely knew each other. "Without question. I'll even make you a certificate. *Jonathan Allen. Hartley Farren's Favorite Person.*"

That crooked smile emerged again, and hope flooded through her. "Hmm. I don't know. I mean, a certificate is nice and all, but..."

Hartley braced her hands on her hips. "Are you teasing me? Because that would be evil, Jonathan, and you don't strike me as an evil man." Now *she* arched a brow.

His chuckle this time was different. Deeper. Grittier. Sexier. With an undercurrent of...something she didn't understand. "You never know, Hartley."

Her stomach did a little flip, because it had been eons since anyone had flirted with her. Or, at least, since she'd allowed herself to notice. Let alone a man this attractive. "Oh, come on. Can I at least tell you what my favor is?" she asked.

Those gray eyes sparkled with amusement. "Well, I couldn't help but overhear your phone conversation, so I have an inkling."

Wait. He *knew* what she needed and still hadn't said no? Hope and anticipation rushed through her, making her feel restless and brave. "Then if my awesome certificate idea isn't enough, what can I offer to convince you to walk out to my slip and take a look at my catamaran?"

That eyebrow arched again, and Hartley suddenly felt like they'd been playing chess—and her words had just allowed him to put her in checkmate. But still, he didn't make any claims of her.

She stepped closer and dared to flirt back. "Jonathan. Mr. Allen. *Mr. Allen, My Already Officially Favorite Person*, are you going to make me beg? Because that wouldn't be very nice," she added playfully.

Those gray eyes flared. She would've sworn they did. He bit back a chuckle as he shook his head. And when his words came, they were filled with a deep intensity that made her shiver. "Why don't you show me your boat, Hartley, and then I'll answer your questions."

Want More Hot Contemporary Romance from Laura Kaye?

CHECK OUT:

The Raven Riders Series –
A motorcycle club with a protective mission...
Brotherhood. Club. Family.
They live and ride by their own rules.
These are the Raven Riders . . .

RIDE HARD (RAVEN RIDERS #1)

Raven Riders Motorcycle Club President Dare Kenyon rides hard and values loyalty above all else. He'll do anything to protect the brotherhood of bikers—the only family he's got—as well as those who can't defend themselves. So when beautiful but mistrustful Haven Randall lands on the club's doorstep scared that she's being hunted, Dare takes her in, swears to keep her safe, and pushes to learn the secrets overshadowing her pretty smile before it's too late.

RIDE ROUGH (RAVEN RIDERS #2)

Alexa Harmon thought she had it all—the security of a good job, a beautiful home, and a powerful, charming fiancé who offered the life she never had growing up. But when her dream quickly turns into a nightmare, Alexa realizes she's fallen for a façade she can't escape—until her ex-boyfriend and Raven Riders MC vice-president Maverick Ryland offers her a way out. Forced together to keep Alexa safe, their powerful attraction reignites and Maverick determines to do whatever it takes to earn a second chance—one Alexa is tempted to give. But her ex-fiancé isn't going to let her go without a fight, one that will threaten everything they both hold dear.

RIDE WILD (RAVEN RIDERS #3)

Wild with grief over the death of his wife, Sam "Slider" Evans merely lives for his two sons. Nothing holds his interest anymore—not even riding his bike or his membership in the Raven Riders Motorcycle Club. But then he hires Cora Campbell to be his nanny. Cora adores Slider's sweet boys, but never expected the red-hot attraction to their brooding, sexy father. If only he would notice her... Slider does see the beautiful, fun-loving woman he invited into his home. She makes him feel *too* much, and he both hates it and yearns for it. But when Cora witnesses something she shouldn't have, the new lives they've only just discovered are threatened. Now Slider must claim—and protect—what's his before it's too late.

RIDE DIRTY (RAVEN RIDERS #3.5)

Caine McKannon is all about rules. As the Raven Riders Sergeant-at-Arms, he prizes loyalty to his brothers and protection of his club. As a man, he takes pleasure wherever he can get it but allows no one close—because distance is the only way to ensure people can't hurt you. And he's had enough pain for a lifetime. But then he rescues a beautiful woman from an attack. Kids and school are kindergarten teacher Emma Kerry's whole life, so she's stunned to realize she has an enemy—and even more surprised to find a protector in the intimidating man who saved her. Tall, dark, and tattooed, Caine is unlike any man Emma's ever known, and she's as uncertain of him as she is attracted. As the danger escalates, Caine is in her house more and more – until one night of passion lands him in her bed. But breaking the rules comes at a price, forcing Caine to fight dirty to earn a chance at love.

THE HARD INK SERIES

Five dishonored soldiers
Former Special Forces
One last mission
These are the men of Hard Ink…

HARD AS IT GETS (HARD INK #1)

Trouble just walked into Nicholas Rixey's tattoo parlor. Becca Merritt is warm, sexy, wholesome—pure temptation to a very jaded Nick. He's left his military life behind to become co-owner of Hard Ink Tattoo, but Becca is his ex-commander's daughter. Loyalty won't let him turn her away. Lust has plenty to do with it too. With her brother presumed kidnapped, Becca needs Nick. She just wasn't expecting to want him so much. As their investigation turns into all-out war with an organized crime ring, only Nick can protect her. And only Becca can heal the scars no one else sees.

HARD AS YOU CAN (HARD INK #2)

Shane McCallan doesn't turn his back on a friend in

need, especially a former Special Forces teammate running a dangerous, off-the-books operation. Nor can he walk away from Crystal, the gorgeous blonde waitress is hiding secrets she doesn't want him to uncover. Too bad. He's exactly the man she needs to protect her sister, her life, and her heart. All he has to do is convince her that when something feels this good, you hold on as hard as you can—and never let go.

Hard to Hold On To (Hard Ink #2.5)

Edward "Easy" Cantrell knows better than most the pain of not being able to save those he loves—which is why he is not going to let Jenna Dean, the woman he helped rescue from a gang, out of his sight. He may have just met her, but Jenna's the first person to make him feel alive since that devastating day in the desert more than a year ago. As the pair are thrust together while chaos reigns around them, they both know one thing: the things in life most worth having are the hardest to hold on to.

Hard to Come By (Hard Ink #3)

When a sexy stranger asks questions about her brother, Emilie Garza is torn between loyalty to the brother she once idolized and fear of the war-changed man he's become. Derek DiMarzio's easy smile and quiet strength tempt Emilie to open up, igniting the desire between them and leading Derek to crave a woman he shouldn't trust. Now, Derek and Emilie must prove where their loyalties lie before hearts are broken and lives are lost. Because love is too hard to come by to let slip away…

Hard to Be Good (Hard Ink #3.5)

Hard Ink Tattoo owner Jeremy Rixey has taken on his

brother's stateside fight against the forces that nearly killed Nick and his Special Forces team a year before. Now, Jeremy's whole world has been turned upside down—not the least of which by kidnapping victim Charlie Merritt, a brilliant, quiet blond man who tempts Jeremy to settle down for the first time ever. With tragedy and chaos all around them, temptation flashes hot, and Jeremy and Charlie can't help but wonder why they're trying so hard to be good...

HARD TO LET GO (HARD INK #4)

Beckett Murda hates to dwell on the past. But his investigation into the ambush that killed half his Special Forces team and ended his Army career gives him little choice. Just when his team learns how powerful their enemies are, hard-ass Beckett encounters his biggest complication yet—his friend's younger sister, seductive, feisty Katherine Rixey. When Kat joins the fight, she lands straight in Beckett's sights . . . and in his arms. Not to mention their enemies' crosshairs. Now Beckett and Kat must set aside their differences to work together, because the only thing sweeter than justice is finding love and never letting go.

HARD AS STEEL (HARD INK #4.5, RAVEN RIDERS #.5)

After identifying her employer's dangerous enemies, Jessica Jakes takes refuge at the compound of the Raven Riders Motorcycle Club. Fellow Hard Ink tattooist and Raven leader Ike Young promises to keep Jess safe for as long as it takes, which would be perfect if his close, personal, round-the-clock protection didn't make it so hard to hide just how much she wants him—and always has. The last thing Ike needs is alone time with the sexiest woman he's ever known, one he's purposely kept at a distance for years. Now, Ike's not sure he can keep his hands or his heart to himself—or that he even wants to anymore.

Hard Ever After (Hard Ink #5)

After a long battle to discover the truth, the men and women of Hard Ink have a lot to celebrate, especially the wedding of two of their own—Nick Rixey and Becca Merritt, whose hard-fought love deserves a happy ending. But an old menace they thought long gone reemerges, threatening the peace they've only just found. Now, for one last time, Nick and Becca must fight for their always and forever.

Hard to Serve (Hard Ink #5.5/Blasphemy #.5)

To protect and serve is all Detective Kyler Vance ever wanted to do, so when Internal Affairs investigates him as part of the new police commissioner's bid to oust corruption, everything is on the line. Which makes meeting smart, gorgeous submissive, Mia Breslin, at an exclusive play club the perfect distraction. Their scorching scenes lure them to play together again and again. But then Kyler runs into Mia at work and learns that he's been dominating the daughter of the hard-ass boss who has it in for him. Now Kyler must choose between life-long duty and forbidden desire before Mia finds another who's not so hard to serve.

THE HEARTS IN DARKNESS DUET –
A sexy and emotional strangers-to-lovers story...

Hearts in Darkness
(Hearts in Darkness Duet #1)

Two strangers. Four hours. One pitch-black elevator.

Makenna James thinks her day can't get any worse, until she finds herself stranded in a pitch-black elevator with a complete stranger. Caden Grayson is amused when a harried redhead dashes into his elevator fumbling her bags and cell phone, but his amusement turns to panic when the power fails. Despite his piercings, tats, and vicious scar, he's terrified of the dark and confined spaces. Now, he's trapped in his own worst nightmare. To fight fear, they must reach out and open up. With no preconceived notions based on looks to hold them back, they discover just how much they have in common. In the warming darkness, attraction grows and sparks fly, but will they feel the same when the lights come back on?

Love in the Light
(Hearts in Darkness Duet #2)

Two hearts in the darkness...must fight for love in the light...

Makenna James and Caden Grayson have been inseparable since the day they were trapped in a pitch-black elevator and found acceptance and love in the arms of a stranger. Makenna hopes that night put them on the path to forever—which can't happen until she introduces her tattooed, pierced, and scarred boyfriend to her father and three over-protective brothers. Haunted by a childhood tragedy and the loss of his family, Caden never thought he'd find the love he shares with Makenna. But the deeper he falls, the more he fears the devastation sure to come if he ever lost her, too. When meeting her family doesn't go smoothly, Caden questions whether Makenna deserves someone better, stronger, and just more...normal. Maybe they're just too different—and he's far too damaged—after all…

THE HEROES SERIES – Two best friends, two military heroes, two epic love stories…

HER FORBIDDEN HERO (HEROES #1)

Former Army Special Forces Sgt. Marco Vieri has never thought of Alyssa Scott as more than his best friend's little sister, but her return home changes that...and challenges him to keep his war-borne demons at bay. Marco's not the same person he was back when he protected Alyssa from her abusive father, and he's not about to let her see the mess he's become. But Alyssa's not looking for protection—not anymore. Now that she's back in his life, she's determined to heal her forbidden hero one touch at a time...

ONE NIGHT WITH A HERO (HEROES #2)

After growing up with an abusive, alcoholic father, Army Special Forces Sgt. Brady Scott vowed never to marry or have kids. Sent stateside to get his head on straight—and his anger in check—Brady's looking for a distraction. He finds it in Joss Daniels, his beautiful new neighbor whose one-night-only offer for hot sex leads to more. Suddenly, Brady's not so sure he can stay away. But when Joss discovers she's pregnant, Brady's rejection leaves her feeling abandoned. Now, they must overcome their fears before they lose the love and security they've found in each other, but can they let go of the past to create a future together?

About Laura Kaye

Laura is the New York Times and USA Today bestselling author of over thirty books in contemporary and erotic romance and romantic suspense, including the Blasphemy, Hard Ink, and Raven Riders series. Growing up, Laura's large extended family believed in the supernatural, and family lore involving angels, ghosts, and evil-eye curses cemented in Laura a life-long fascination with storytelling and all things paranormal. Laura also writes historical fiction as the NYT bestselling author, Laura Kamoie. She lives in Maryland with her husband and two daughters and appreciates her view of the Chesapeake Bay every day.

Learn more and join Laura's VIP Readers at LauraKayeAuthor.com